T0105707

SWORD OF SALVATION

KENT BRINDLEY

WestBow
PRESS
A DIVISION OF THOMAS NELSON

ISBN: 978-1-4497-7808-8 (sc)
ISBN: 978-1-4497-7809-5 (e)
ISBN: 978-1-4497-7810-1 (hc)

Library of Congress Control Number: 2012922795

WestBow Press books may be ordered through booksellers or by contacting:

WestBow Press
A Division of Thomas Nelson
1663 Liberty Drive
Bloomington, IN 47403
www.westbowpress.com
1-(866) 928-1240

Printed in the United States of America

WestBow Press rev. date: 12/03/2012

To family and friends who have supported me along the way. "Teamwork makes the dream work."

"And take the helmet of salvation, and the sword of the Spirit, which is the word of God" (Ephesians 6:17; NKJV)

Contents

THE FELLOWSHIP UNITES

PROLOGUE

Beyond a distant star rests the lost planet, Trina. It is a realm of lush valleys, running streams, grand mountain ranges, and brilliant sunrises. On a world of such luscious beauty, serenity abounds from shore to shore. Creatures of land, sea, and air coexist in peace and prosperity.

Then came the day that humanity discovered Trina's shores with its lush landscape, possible riches…and likewise opportunity to cultivate this new world amongst blameless creatures who would never protect themselves. Hence, as the settlers descended upon Trina, they arrived in two warring factions.

As the founding settlers arrived on Trina, the pioneers dedicated its land under the auspices of religious principle. The belief in a Great Authority governing their speech and actions guided the people to an unshakable belief that all that they ever said and did made them noble and righteous. All that they needed do was keep their actions, thoughts and speech dictated by loose translations of the Sacred Text. Seeing that the words, thoughts, and actions of the righteous were always correct, anyone who disagreed required additional guidance; at any cost. The bravest and most divine missionaries set out on missions extended toward the indoctrination of those who would arrive in their footsteps.

As the religious went out to petition new arrivals, they were introduced to the idea of the unreligious; equally devout, if equally stubborn, in their belief that they represented their own authority. As paths were crossed with the unreligious, it was not long before religious missions were viewed with a sense of contempt and offense. Still, the religious were determined to spread their guidance at any cost.

The Great War separating neighbors and even family members was the result. The unreligious sought to silence the notions of persecutions with swords and spears. The religious responded in kind and soon delivered fewer empathetic verses to convert the unreligious and delivered more spears and tridents to silence the oppression instead. The last differentiating factor between the two factions of settlers was gone; either side was more than willing to go to war for their cause.

As years turned to generations to centuries, the Great War pressed on. Children born to the governing religious continued to promise to work toward ministry through family interpretations of the Sacred Text. Those born of the unbeliever vowed for the end of religious persecution. Messages of ministry from either spectrum gave way to violence begetting violence for enough generations that no one remembered what the fight represented anymore. Beneath a hatred and suspicion of neighbors that could not have come from man, the war pressed on. Only one man could fight the evil guiding the actions of both sides in the Great War.

JOVAN

The sun rise over Trina's capital city of Krill revealed a crowd standing before the edge of a great hill. The crowd had separated into two lines of equal proportions by necessity. The Elves, in all of their majesty, presided over one line and carried many copies of the Sacred Text, the words of their Great Authority. The Dwarves remained relegated to the opposite line, grumbling and spitting upon the idea of the dictations of some mistranslation of a Sacred Text. The misinterpretation of the division of power by some Grandiose King had carried on for too long through history. For all of the differences that the separate factions boasted, two things remained the same: both factions were backed by human support and had brought their weapons. For that particular moment, those weapons were placed in two separate piles a few inches away in mutual understanding. Both factions were only gathered to gaze upon one person.

Atop the hill, Mother Superior Martilla Bourg stood impressed by the sight below. The people of Trina had placed aside their differences in the interest of being presented with her son, Trina's recorded champion. As she absorbed all of the attention brought to her house, the Elder turned away from the crowd to face the mansion. Her family's home and her home away from the church stood gated, sheltered, and bare. Then, her all-encompassing, sweeping glance fell upon the meditating form at the door of the barn stables.

Joto was dressed in his lime green tunic, matching leggings, and crimson cape. He wore not the traditional boots of a rancher but straw sandals and a Chinese-inspired shade to match. The shade would have concealed the skeletal face if a mask over the chin did not. The scythes that he toiled with in the field lay to either side of his meditating form. His dagger was barely visible in its sleeve pocket. Resting on the ground at the tireless servant's side was a woven basket concealing his prized katana. Joto was not in the mood to spring to action; he was in the mood to meditate and channel his energies toward a peaceful resolution to this conflict. Still, that peaceful resolution hadn't come in generations and wouldn't arrive over night. Trina needed a Savior and Martilla needed to snap her farm servant out of his trance. He had a duty to fetch the hero that Divine Authority had promised Trina.

"It is time for the rivaling people of Trina to meet their mutual Savior." Martilla announced, "Raise the boy."

Joto snapped to consciousness, his shade and mask becoming dislodged just long enough to reveal his skeletal face, beady eyes, and unkempt soul patch. The faithful servant readjusted the cover, uncrossed his legs clumsily, and sprang back to his feet. From his standing position, he collected his back-mounted basket from the ground to keep the katana close at hand while he secured the scythes in the loops of his pants.

"It is early and he must rest, Mother Superior." Joto protested in his high-pitched, overly accented natural speech.

"He is not a child; he is a man destined by Divine Authority to be the Savior that Trina has asked for." Martilla insisted, "Wake my son."

As Martilla's oldest confidant and servant through the church and farm, Joto could have argued the point in all of the divine wisdom that he had acquired over the years. Still, divine wisdom also taught him respect for his elders in authority. Furthermore, his current audience was Mother Superior, not only the church's highest Mother but the boy's mother as well. Joto withdrew a scythe from its belt loop and loosed the lock on the stable doors.

"The savior who resides in stables awaits, Mother Superior." Joto announced.

The mother's lips drew into a thin line at the wry observation. The son of the church's most important leader slept in the stables and bore a brown button-up tunic as though he were a common farming servant. His late father might have been proud to see his son dismiss any pride in the upbringing of the religious in accordance with his humbling lesson; the mother was not.

As Martilla Bourg entered the stables, she nearly tripped over the glistening armor that would have signified her son's radiance as a Soldier of the Cloth. She had gifted him the armor at the request of the parish. It was a generous Divine Gift and Jovan showed the audacity to not accept it. The Icarus Blade, the church heirloom, hung from the wall of the stable, untouched by the recipient's hand. As Bourg entered farther into the stables, she finally did find the sleeping form of the Savior that the world was waiting for. In fact, she nearly tripped over the boy. However, the additional disturbance did wake him and Jovan Bourg sat up amidst the bales of hay on which he had slept. As he wiped from hay from his straw-colored locks, the boy's blue-grey eyes peered out into the darkness at the arriving form of his mother.

"It is time for the public to meet their champion." Martilla announced, stooping to pick up one of the steel boot sheaths that would start his armor. As Jovan placed a hand on his mother's shoulder to stop her and held a shepherd's staff in his free hand, the assurance was made clear.

"Then the good people of Trina shall meet a Savior who is adorned as one of them." Jovan observed in a murmur of humble baritone. With that, he rose up and stepped past the Mother of the Church. He was not adorned not as a Son of the Cloth or knight of royalty. He bore the fashions of the unlearned to go and greet the people who had waited for his rising.

Martilla shook her head somberly as her son left the stables in a tunic and worker's slacks and without so much as a shower--all because his father had confused taking pride in his religious identity with being boastful. Jovan had been summoned as Trina's Savior to prevent the war from going on longer than it had to. To be entrusted with such a great mission, he should have felt honored. Yet Jovan passed right by the armor and blade identifying him as the one true Knight of Salvation on his way out of the stables. He did, however, secure a crystalline crucifix around his neck and accepted a crimson cape from Joto as he was escorted to the edge of the hillside so the crowd could gaze upon the hero whom they had been promised.

Below in the valley, the Elves and their religious followers shared their expectant gaze upon the hillside with the Dwarves and their unreligious loyalists. As the two rivaling factions studiously ignored one another in the understanding that their fighting was still at an uneasy truce, the two groups took in the form materializing on the hillside beneath the rising sun. The people of Trina were equally surprised to gaze upon a boy dressed in the garbs of a simple servant. Had the religious not promised the world this Savior? He dressed as the commoner, and the commoner was understood to be the agitator of antireligious violence.

Even the unreligious regarded the hero presented before them with a sense of suspicion. He dressed as one of them, yet he bore a cross around his neck and carried the Sacred Text. It was only a matter of time before he tried to either convert or kill them. Was this the man that they were expected to worship as Trina's saving grace? As the Elves and the believers murmured amongst one another in doubt that Jovan Bourg was truly the savior for the religious that the Sacred Text had spoken of, the Dwarves and unreligious peoples whispered their plans to prevent Bourg of the Religious from slaying them by the blade in their sleep.

The whispers and murmurs of the ages old enemies reached the hillside on a strong breeze of doubt and suspicion. Martilla Bourg hung back outside the crowd's collective gaze and hung her head pathetically. Her son, the representative for the family and church, was presenting himself as an unwashed buffoon rather than as the predestined Knight of Salvation. Joto, servant to the cross, stood at Jovan's side and urged the boy to speak. Still, Jovan gave pause until the din from below in the valley had quieted itself. Whoever this was, whatever his true destiny, and whichever end he truly served, he commanded attention.

"Fetch me the Icarus." Jovan instructed. Instantly, Martilla presented her son with the blade. The boy finally understood his destiny and accepted it with pride.

Jovan raised the mighty Icarus high over his head for all to see. The believers applauded the gesture as a declaration of war; the nonbelievers narrowed their eyes, suspicious of a declaration of sneak attack. With a flourish, Jovan dug the Icarus's blade into the ground and the sunlight reflected off of the weapon's hilt. The Icarus resembled no weapon, but a radiant cross on the hillside in its stead.

The "cross" remained on the hillside to cast its radiant glow over all of Krill from that sunrise to the following sunset. Gazing upon such a sight, the people in the valley remained paralyzed with awe, their weapons neglected. The glistening war-blade cross; was this a sign of hope? Or a secret signal to pursue religious oppression in the name of self-righteousness? Though the fighting and weapon bearing had been put on hold for the first time in generations, the harsh murmurings were evidence enough of just how great the divide truly was on Trina's shores.

Martilla Bourg approached the Icarus several times in hopes of uprooting it and restoring it to the Knight of Salvation. However, she could not draw near the blade. Joto, her most loyal subject, guarded the cross from his mistress's hand. Clearly, only one could decide when it was time to raise the blade in defense of religion once more. Martilla abandoned the restless crowd to their devices and turned on her heels to approach not the beautiful mansion adjacent to the church where the family slept. No; her destination was the stables where her stubborn mule of a son hung his head in humility. As the Mother Superior of the church left the crowd and entered the stables, she did not have to make her pilgrimage alone. Viscar Halas, a valuable missionary soldier, was summoned out of the crowd. Dutifully, the respected captain collected his trident and net before making the pilgrimage out of the valley and up the hill to his Mother Superior's side.

Within the stables that Jovan humbled himself as viewing as home, the boy had already placed on the sheaths, gauntlets, and armor. The garb's radiance, revealed wherever he rode, was not to be mistaken. Before the armor was complete, the boy tied his straw-colored hair tight and reached for the helmet that would hide the identity of a mere boy or any other mortal. The swift, strong, noble, predestined Knight of Salvation would have no human identity of his own until the day came that the evil was driven out of Trina. As Jovan began lowering the helmet over his head, the door swung open to reveal the company of Martilla Bourg and Viscar Halas, her church's prized "missionary" soldier.

"My son, please listen to—OH!" Martilla declared, gazing upon the armored form presented before her, "You are preparing to take this pilgrimage?"

"Was I not destined to do so?" the timid baritone echoed through the helmet, "I am saddling up Danavas for the harsh journey ahead. I will raise up the Icarus at sunset and be off in the morrow."

"You are the better man than I to take this fight to its source, young lord." Halas applauded, collapsing to bended knee in the middle of the stable, "Fear not. We will not abandon our duties to deliver from the Sacred Text while you are gone."

Jovan glowered beneath his helmet at the dark-haired, fair faced soldier kneeling at his feet with his trident and net with no Sacred Text in sight.

"From where I stand, confused Viscar," he observed, "you appear intent on delivering a trident and net."

Mother Superior stood shocked by her son's vicious criticisms toward not only a member of the enlightened but the greatest ally that the church had to offer in the field. Viscar Halas, the church's most valuable soldier, remained knelt at the holy knight's feet but his eyes registered confusion.

"Young Lord, I don't—" Viscar began, swallowing sheepishly, "—understand what you are saying, I'm afraid."

Jovan gazed upon the sheepish form of the mighty missionary soldier. Mother Superior glared at her son beneath that armor in demand of an apology. Jovan removed the helmet to reveal his true face once more. There stood the face of Martilla Bourg's son in all of his sincerity.

"Rise, noble friend of the Church." Bourg requested.

Viscar obediently rose from his prostrate state of profound servitude on trembling knees. Utilizing his trident for stability, the simple missionary rose to meet the unarmored face of the predestined holy Knight of Salvation.

"You speak only of a desire to share enlightenment from the Sacred

Text." Jovan continued, settling a comforting hand on his ally's shoulder, "I merely asked why you carried no copy of the Sacred Text but weapons in its stead."

"We are at *war*, my son!" Mother Superior interjected, sharply, "It is all that the unenlightened understand!"

"What does the church understand?" Jovan asked, his tone suggesting patience as he tended to Danavas, slinging an armored saddle over the steed's snow white form and silver mane.

Martilla Bourg narrowed her eyes coldly at the youth. Mother Superior would never accept being spoken to in such a manner; not even by the Son of the Cloth and especially not right in front of the church's most valuable missionary. With the conversation clearly over, the crowd required tending to before another conflict broke out. Mother Superior left the stables, accompanied by Viscar to attend to the peace in his own group. Jovan Bourg was left alone in the stables once more to prepare for his coming. Still, Knight of Salvation or no, there was no reason that he should have to face the forthcoming trials alone...

Under the watchful gaze of Martilla Bourg and Joto, the two rivaling factions grew restless. They had assembled together at sun up to greet their Knight of Salvation and had not lifted a single finger in war all day. Then, the crowds were only greeted, for the better part of the day, with the loudest voices for the believers. The unreligious were griping rightfully; the religious were just as rightly offended by the complaints. Then, before the first blow was cast against Viscar's better judgment, the shadows of a steed and armored rider fell over the crowds.

"The Sacred Text speaks of one Knight of Salvation." The rider announced in humble baritone, "It also speaks of a gathered Trinity. I shall assemble this Trinity to aid me in my course."

The murmurings of tension became expressions of acclamation. The Great War would be ceased by not only one man; one man might find himself susceptible to temptations on a long and tumultuous journey. Trina would be freed from the terrors of war by a Great Trinity *and* a Knight of Salvation!

"Who is this Trinity that the Sacred Text speaks of, Mother Superior?"

asked a voice of one of the church elders, "Surely, such a Fellowship would defend the church from this upheaval!"

"Or free the good people of Trina from the church's iron grasp!" Darath Noar, the appointed voice of the unbelievers, corrected him. A cry of approval came from the unbelievers and the believers reached not for their Sacred Texts but their weapons in consternation.

Mother Superior did not know how to respond. The Sacred Text had spoken many times of a Great Trinity; but it had never identified its members or how they would come. It certainly never spoke of them working together *with* the Knight of Salvation. In fact, they were mentioned in separate sections of the Sacred Text. As Mother Superior grew flustered, her son, the Knight of Salvation, rested a comforting hand on her shoulder. He could field this question.

"I will select this Trinity; a great Fellowship of otherwise ordinary people destined to observe me on my quest and steer me from the same temptations that Trina has fallen to."

Jovan would select the members of the Trinity fellowship himself. That was all that the crowd needed to know. The nervous murmur rose to cries of suggestion as to who should join Jovan on his quest. Only as the Knight of Salvation unearthed the Icarus Blade once more and raised it to the heavens did the din silence itself again in anticipation.

"*I* will make my choices as to whom I will trust to keep me on the righteous path in the coming days." Jovan insisted.

With that, the two rivaling groups collected their weapons and trudged back to their homes. In the morning, the bitter war would persist and the soldiers for both sides needed to be rested up. As the crowd dispersed, Jovan turned Danavas around toward the stables. As horse and rider turned, they were greeted by Mother Superior, Joto, and Viscar, his weapons restored.

"Select Joto for this quest." Mother Superior offered, "He has served the church and this family well for many years. His sage wisdom will be a great asset."

"Also take with you my weapons and loyalty to the church." Viscar added.

"Joto's sage wisdom is needed here in hopes of leading the church, and Viscar still needs to lead the army so long as this war continues. Perhaps he might lead them toward a sense of peaceful ministry as I have suggested." Jovan announced, turning back to gaze out over the fields. "I know what I am to do on this quest…"

With that, Jovan Bourg left his home as the Knight of Salvation. As Danavas trotted down the hillside amidst gazes of praise, it was his rider who was greeted with shouts of acclamation. As the crowd separated to either side out of respect for the path of horse and rider, the rider did the unthinkable and removed his helmet to reveal the face of a fellow man. Whatever evil force had continued to dictate the war and drive old ill will in both factions, it was still a fellow man who was destined to confront such an evil and destroy it. Even the Son of the Church, in all of his righteousness, was still only human.

Upon observing the Knight of Salvation, it was anticipated that the fellowship of three would follow him down the hill on his quest. He had, after all, already selected Joto, the sage, Viscar, the missionary soldier, and a third from the church to fill out the ranks. Still, no other rider followed to the chants of commendation from the crowd. Furthermore, Joto remained rooted on his spot on the hill and Viscar stood alongside his army of the religious, discarding his weapons at his feet for but another moment and carrying the Sacred Text in an expression of solidarity.

"Friends," a barely audible timbre of humble baritone demanded the crowd's attention as the rider dismounted his steed and placed himself on the level of his supporters, "I have promised you a Holy Trinity to help aid me in my quest. However, the Sacred Text has not identified their members. I will make those selections of my own accord. Be well, friends of Krill."

With that, Jovan remounted Danavas and trotted away amidst the murmurs of the religious and unreligious. Who would this Holy Trinity be? And why had the Sacred Text not recorded their identities…?

ARMIN

Blessed with ethereal beauty and many talents, the Elven Lords of Dawn Valley and the mountain landscapes of Tress practiced thankful observance. Though a few of the Elves exercised great personal pride in all of their blessings, others dedicated their praises to the glory of the Great King. It remained, however, a degree of pride that many would question if the Elves would extend to the Great Almighty if they were not as physically beautiful or as greatly talented. Nevertheless, as the Elven Lords stood, they remained the loudest voices for the believers, preaching louder than many human ministers of peace.

Amidst the Elven Lords of Dawn Valley was their ruling class blessed by the Great Almighty to rule with the same grace as a long line of kings. Every member of the royal lineage of Oran Kinston was blessed with a greater ethereal beauty than any of their followers and with a natural prestige and grace. When a member of such a royal linage addressed their Elven brothers, the lower castes took heed with a great sense of respect. When the Elven Lords addressed other feudal lords, the true believing kings listened as well. Only the cursed, jealous nonbelievers would not heed the wisdom offered by the Elf Lords; they could be enlightened in due time. Only one member of the Kinston bloodline did not seem destined for the throne.

Armin Kinston, brought into the royal lineage by adoption, shared in the family's complexion but not their natural ability to lead. What he was blessed with was a supernatural ability with swords and especially with a bow. Armin was blessed as the great hunter and afforded much attention from his peers. His unnatural eyesight, hearing, and sense of his surroundings gave him the skills of a great hunter. His golden bow and arsenal of arrows made him unbeatable. In swordsmanship, his blades were indestructible and his speed and agility allowed him to dodge any attacker. Nonetheless, he was not of royal blood and not observed with their respect

As a hunter, the day that stands out most in Armin's mind was the day of his own birthday celebration. He had been implored by the royal family to hunt the meat for his birthday dinner. As a reward for Armin's efforts, he had tracked a glorious buck complete with a rack of golden horns. As Armin returned to the palace grounds with his prize catch, however, he was stopped at the gates with some of the less important guests. Inside of the kingdom, the sounds of a grand celebration penetrated the early evening air. Kinston, the guest of honor at his birthday, struggled his way forward to the front of the line, carrying the succulent feast. Within moments, the gates were opened to the mighty, cunning hunter and the grand feast was taken inside by two palace attendants. The gates were then promptly slammed in Armin Kinston's face, abandoning the guest of honor at the palace gates with the lowest castes. The sounds of great celebration continued out into the night air, enticing the crowd gathered at the gates to remain standing in case they should be decreed as acceptable to enter. Still, the crowd would not stay rooted by their hopes of recognition from the royal family. Armin was not viewed as true royalty and the royal family had not only sent him to stalk his own birthday meal but would not allow him inside to partake of the celebration. Still, there were plenty assembled outside with the great hunter to celebrate at his side.

Deep within the heart of Dawn Valley, just at the foot of Tress Mountains, the sun was just beginning to rise. The realm of Elves was graced with an ethereal beauty that surpassed even the physical beauty of the Elf Lords. As harvest time fell upon the realm of beauty set aside for only the Elves by Holy Decree, many of the Elven Lords assembled in their valleys and fields to celebrate all that they had been graced with by noble birth and give thanks to the Great Almighty for all of their ethereal beauty. It was a well-known fact that this was the harvest time celebration to only be observed by the elves without disturbance from human outsiders. Even the humans who shared in the spiritual gifts of the Elves did not share in their physical beauty. Therefore, no one of human blood was so blessed as to share in their celebration.

Oran Kinston, the supreme Elven Lord, rose up to make the great speech before his gathered followers. Moments before he opened his mouth to speak and sing the praises that the Elves had been blessed with so much more beauty than so many other species and for their glorious harvest, he gave pause as his followers gazed behind him rather than upon him as their ruler. The Elven Lord turned to face the shadow of a horse and rider mounting Tress Mountain. The rider did not appear to be Elven by blood but there he was, disturbing the proceedings of the honorary harvest festival. The Great Almighty would have never directed a human into Dawn Valley without Holy Decree and certainly never during harvest time. Oran Kinston narrowed his eyes from his platform, backed by the twins of royal birth and Armin. As Oran narrowed his eyes at the intruder and summoned the guards flanking the platform, the other Elven Lords gazed up in awestruck wonder. The horse was a creature of silver and snow white beauty beneath his armor. As for its rider, he glistened in the sunrise like a waiflike knight, bearing a blade that closely resembled a radiant cross of Salvation. Despite their stupor, the guards started toward the horse and rider. As Oran recognized the rider, however, he waved off his loyal followers and knelt in the middle of the platform before the intruders. The royal family soon followed suit. Then, watching the most holy leaders kneel before the horse and rider, the other Elves followed suit. If the Elves had been blessed by blood with much physical appearance and many talents, there was one HUMAN whom had been decreed to be the Knight of Salvation on a war-torn world.

"Jovan, Son of Bourg." Oran announced from his knelt position, "We were not expecting your visit during our celebration of the harvest. Please, what brings you here?"

The glistening, armored rider dismounted his steed and indicated to Danavas to stay upon the hill as he approached the crowd of Elven Lords within Dawn Valley. As the Knight of Salvation approached, he promptly removed his helmet once more. His tired blue-grey eyes and straw-colored, shoulder length locks did not demand much attention. The soft-spoken baritone timbre would not draw too much attention to his cause either. Still, the Elves understood and respected Divine Authority.

"Elven Lords of Dawn Valley," Jovan declared, kneeling alongside the platform, "rise. It is I who am visiting you in your land."

Stunned, the Elven Lords recovered their footing. The Knight of Salvation, the highest-most minister of the faith and Savior of Trina, was recognizing the borders that divided nations. Once the Elven Lords were back on their feet, Jovan Bourg began speaking once more before the first murmur of confusion could escape the crowd.

"I am here in search of but the first member of the Fellowship of three who shall support me in my holy quest and keep me on the proper path." Bourg announced.

"You have indeed come to the proper place to discover the suitable followers of faith to keep you on your path!" Oran declared, "Why, standing before you are two great warriors and trappers, my son and daughter, Kinik and Luciana! Or perhaps a great series of tests of proof as to whom should partake in your quest are in order?"

"You speak of Kinik and Luciana as great hunters and warriors." Jovan observed, "Yet, I gaze upon Armin, the one who is heralded across many nations as the greatest in both disciplines?"

"Armin is not of natural royal blood; his presence does not yield a significant respect." Oran insisted, quickly, "You require the best to aid you in this quest; and the best should yield the most respect."

"Agreed." Jovan conceded, "You had spoken of the suggestion of a series of tests as *evidence* as to who has earned their spot in this quest?"

"It shall be a part of our celebration of harvest time!" Oran declared, turning once again to face the crowd of his own followers, "Jovan Bourg will be recognized as our guest for the duration of this celebration!"

The traditional ceremonies marking the arrival of the harvest time in Dawn Valley, traditions passed down since generations before, were forgotten. The ceremonial speeches of thanksgiving, lavish feasts, music, and dancing that were commonly observed were all well and good; but such a ceremony was unbefitting for the observance of Jovan Bourg, the Son of the Church and Knight of Salvation. Besides, many trials and games to test feats of strength, speed, agility, and intelligence would only serve to prove to the Great Almighty just how blessed the Elven race truly was by His righteous hand. Further, it would serve as evidence as to why the Elves deserved to fill out the Trinity. Weapons were gathered, uneasy alliances were assembled, and plans were made amidst teammates for when the great games would begin. The murmurs of the crowd, however, did not reach Kinik and Luciana. They were the twins of noble birth; such a team could surely thin out the ranks quickly. After that, whomsoever was the less winded of the two could surely win the favor of the Knight of Salvation with the final crippling blow of humiliation. Nor, however, did Armin appear particularly concerned. He had been adopted into royal splendor, and he maintained the level headed sense of realism to prove it. Noble birth was not going to help Kinik and Luciana any more than the other Elven Lords forming teams was going to help any of them. In the end, only *one* would accompany the Knight of Salvation on his quest. Armin knelt silently on the platform and checked his quiver with his arsenal of custom arrows, his magnificent golden bow, and his twin blades.

Tension and excitement as Dawn Valley had never experienced before permeated out of the assembled crowds at the feast to mark the renewing of harvest time. Oran Kinston, seated in between his noble-born son and daughter, did everything that he could to keep up the appearances of celebration as much for the benefit of the guest of honor as for the benefit of the castes that he governed over. Still, with an Olympic-inspired game coming up, emotions and tensions were running high. At the end of such a tournament, any team would break down to *one* competitor, dictating Elven Lords on the same team to regard one another with silence and suspicion. It was only a matter of time when the last uneasy alliance would break to one winner; and all of those who lost would do so before the glare of the Knight of Salvation.

When it was clear that the mood governing the year's festivities would not change until the festivities were over, Oran produced a mighty gavel from beneath the head table. It was only as the other Elven Lords were rising to dismiss one another from table that it was made of particular note that Armin Kinston, a member of the royal family, had been relegated to eating alongside the lower castes. Jovan Bourg went to readjust his helmet to be certain that his eyes had not deceived him. Still, before Bourg could get a better view, the gavel came crashing down on the table and the twins of noble birth leapt to attention, their weapons already prepared moments before being dismissed to the first task. There stood the representatives of the royal family, armed with miniature crossbows moments before a race that was designed to test speed and agility.

The first gavel crash had been meant to summon the Elves to attention to approach the starting line; it would be a second gavel crash that would begin the race. Moments before the crowd could disperse, however, the crossbows started firing with the intention of taking out as many of the peasants' legs as possible before the official race even began. It was understood by many of the Elves that such underhanded treachery could only result in a sense of ill will for behavior unbecoming of an Elven Lord. Nonetheless, *all* of the Elves understood that the actions of Kinik and Luciana were governed by the fortunes of noble birth. It was understood by most that any reciprocating action would only result in the peasant's humiliating disqualification before the watchful gaze of the Knight of Salvation.

Then, a flash of gold materialized amidst the crowd and two arrows flew right back through the air aimed right at Kinik and Luciana. Rather, the arrows were aimed at their crossbows and the weapons were promptly taken away from the game.

A dangerous hush fell over the crowd and all eyes scanned the crowd for the culprit whom had taken away the unfair advantage and humbled the twins of royal descent. The members of the crowd would applaud his actions later, perhaps even throw a quiet celebration; but the prince and princess had just been humiliated before the king and the royal guest of honor. In the dead center of the crowd, a fair skinned, blonde Elven archer reslung his magnificent golden bow alongside his quiver of custom designed arrows.

"Lords, ladies," Armin Kinston's soft-spoken timbre announced, indicating down a nearby path, "the starting position of the race is that way."

As the Elven Lords assembled at the starting point to begin the race of speed and agility that would mark the new festivities governing the harvest festival, Oran Kinston hung his head pathetically at the antics displayed by Armin. As the Elven Lords (divided into teams at least for the moment) set off from the starting point, Oran turned to face the Knight of Salvation.

"Jovan, Son of the Church," Oran declared, "I—must apologize for my—for Armin. His actions should not reflect poorly on the true-born noble family."

"The actions that he took this day are certainly worth filing under consideration." The baritone timbre came from beneath the helmet of the Knight of Salvation, rubbing his chin thoughtfully.

As the Elven Lords raced determinedly down the path, everyone knew in the backs of their minds that they were competing against other teams and that in the end, even their own teams would turn against them. As each of the Elves approached the narrow path in between the Lost Bog and Forest of No Tomorrow, however, several teams were shoved into the bog and several others were shoved from behind into the Forest of No Tomorrow to be ensnared by the Iron Vines that tended to grow in the underbrush and on the trees. Thus advanced the team of Kinik and Luciana as the faster and more agile teams were shoved from the course and, therefore, out of the competition.

The royal twins had moved forward in the ranks by treachery. What remained to be seen was who would be the first to betray whom and decide the first member of the accompanying Fellowship early. Moments before exiting the narrow path, however, several golden spikes rained down from above to block the paths of the royal siblings. The regular pathway was blocked; and the side to the left collapsed the twins into the bog while veering right could get them caught in Iron Vines. As the royal twins deliberated who had double-crossed whom and how best to get around the time hazard, a flash of gold and white sailed through the tree tops and out the other side of the narrow path. Armin Kinston, devoid of the respect granted by royal decree but gifted with his own talents, was free to continue on his course amidst the protests of the remaining competitors trapped behind the latest time hazard.

Jovan peered into the monitor crystal to track the race with rapt interest. Oran was watching the same scene unfold and coughed nervously into his palm.

"Treachery decided that race." He grunted. "Knight of Salvation, I promise you; Armin Kinston is a bad egg and clearly not one blessed by noble birth. His actions this day should not deter you from taking an Elven Lord blessed by the Great Almighty with…"

"From where I stand, it was ingenuity, discipline, and natural grace that decided that challenge." Jovan insisted, nodding in satisfaction of what he saw. "This trial was set aside to test speed and agility and Armin Kinston has demonstrated his excellence. Release the other Elven Lords from their snares and summon them back here. I have made my choice."

The sense of peace that embodied Dawn Valley as the blessing over the Elves' homestead was shattered; not so much by the visit from the Knight of Salvation but by the Elven Lords' decision to incite a competition whose victory would surely tear apart families and neighbors with bitterness and jealousy. The Knight of Salvation had graced the harvest in search of the very first member of his Trinity. Then, Oran Kinston had set the decision for a gladiatorial competition that he had nothing to risk in and the ridiculous claim that it had been for Jovan Bourg's benefit rather than his own amusement. There were also the antics of the twins of royalty to take into account; and their father's visible disappointment with the fact that their cheating had not resulted in a guaranteed victory and spot on Jovan's quest. The Elven nobles wanted to congratulate Armin Kinston, an outcast from the throne by adoption and a champion of the everyman through not only his skills but his humility.

The celebratory mood governing the harvest festival was spoiled to bitterness and raw nerves as the failed Elven nobles gathered before the platform upon which Oran, Kinik, and Luciana Kinston seemed to glisten in the setting sun. Alongside the Elven noble lords stood a mere human, not blessed by the Great Almighty with the supreme physical beauty, intellect, or leadership of the Elves. The boy with the straw locks and dim blue-grey eyes even dared to be dressed in a farmer's tunic before gracing the Harvest Festival in the Elven kingdom of Dawn Valley. It was only as the boy rose to speak amidst the murmur of the crowds before him that the Elves spied the silver white armor glistening before their eyes. The unassuming baritone timbre that left his voice was the final descriptor to reveal his identity and silence the crowds. Jovan Bourg, Son of the Church and Knight of Salvation, was still human but certainly worth respect.

As Jovan rose, the elves waited to hear the first declaration from the Knight of Salvation directed at them. Still, there were many moments where he did not speak. Instead, Jovan gazed upon the royal family of three; then back out over the restless crowd.

"Where is Armin Kinston?" Jovan asked in a tone that suggested a simple request.

A blur of white and gold approached the platform from the back of the line, the Elven archer and swordsman's eyes reflecting confusion. These were the first words from the Knight of Salvation to the Elven Lords; a question of what had become of the noble family's best kept secret? The twins appeared equally confused from their places to either side of their father. Oran Kinston's gut reaction only reflected suspicion and uneasiness as the murmur rose up once more.

"Here, Knight of Salvation." Armin announced.

Jovan nodded assent that the answer had been fulfilled.

"Sit with your family, Prince of Elves." Jovan declared, gesturing at an open seat, "You are the first of many who will follow me on my quests to purge beloved Trina of this unseen evil."

Amidst the escalating noise of the crowds, Oran tugged at Jovan's tunic.

"Young Knight of Salvation," Oran murmured, "I do not wish to argue with your edicts but..."

"He has competed with enough integrity this day as to not wish harm upon his fellow competitors. He also exercised great ingenuity to utilize the tree tops as his running grounds and agility in his ability to navigate his chosen path." Jovan insisted, "Further, he is regarded as royalty outside of noble birth. While royalty demands respect, his lack of noble birth has cemented a sense of humility in his life that your commoners have grown to appreciate."

The murmur from the crowd became a pronouncement of accolades from the commoners who had grown to respect Armin with the knowledge that they had his respect. Still, the same pronouncement of accolades did not come from the royal crowd hosting the gathering. With the slightest gesture from their king, Oran's guards dispersed the crowds back to their homes. The festivities were over for the day. With the crowds gone, the ruler took Jovan aside in confidence.

"Forgive me, Son of the Church; you've chosen a peasant missionary and archer to assist in a mission petitioned by the Great Almighty." Oran declared, "My son, Kinik; he would be glad to accompany you. He is strong with a sword. Or beauteous Luciana; she would gladly watch *personally* over your quest and is faithful of heart."

"Then they are needed here with their own kind so long as the threat of war still exists." Jovan insisted, "You call Armin a simple missionary. I will require spiritual guidance before this mission is over. You claim him to be an archer. I will need the protection of the weapon held by the man long famed as the *best* archer. Of course, the decision to bear the cross of such a quest at my side is ultimately yours, dutiful archer."

Armin was torn by the conflicting messages. He had been told each day by his royal host family that he amounted to nothing save for a simple peasant. However, the Elven kind outside of the palace halls heralded him as a person of importance. Furthermore, the offer, presented directly from Jovan Bourg, to not only join his journey but that he would watch over the Knight of Salvation added to a sense of grandeur that Armin Kinston did not necessarily mind.

The Knight of Salvation, armored and astride faithful Danavas, led Armin and his light brown mount, Swift, out of Dawn Valley early the next morning. As the pair rode through the Valley, ending Jovan's visit and scheduling harvest time to continue as it had always been celebrated, the crowds gathered outside of their homes once more to see off their local hero. Armin Kinston blushed red in his fair-skinned face in spite of himself beneath his shoulder-length blonde mane. Still, he decided to dodge mentioning such grandeur aloud.

"Swift is a very important steed, no?" Armin asked, loud enough for the crowd to hear him humble himself.

"He carries a very important rider, my friend." Jovan insisted, "Press forward."

Behind Jovan, and before the crowds, Armin caught himself beaming with pride. The declaration of his importance was a new sensation for him and he was not going to lie and declare that he did not appreciate it. As Armin beamed with pride at the declaration of the rider's importance, his renewed countenance of pride was wryly observed by the Knight of Salvation.

HELIMSLYNCH

The Dwarven folk resided deep in the core of the mines of the Iron Mountains. The Dwarves retained great pride in their brute physical strength in combat, certainly enough to make up for their short stature, and their abilities as blacksmiths. Thus allowed them great advantages in the oncoming war. The molten core of Iron Mountain provided the dwarves with many opportunities as weaponsmiths. There had been a time when they had thanklessly developed weapons and items for their human brothers. However, those days long since passed.

The Grandiose King that the Sacred Text spoke of, and the church promptly misrepresented, had sentenced the Dwarves to a stature that cast them aside as laughable outcasts wherever they went outside of Iron Mountain. Only amongst the other Dwarves were they accepted, indicating a shared curse. The idea seemed a little ridiculous to most; but if the Elven Lords could boast of such a Great Almighty who had forged them to look as they did, then the Dwarf Lords could curse the same Grandiose King. Especially when the church leaders and other human agents consistently laughed in the Dwarf Lords faces for their looks and cast them back home into the Iron Mountains with only one another as allies. Even the warriors of the unreligious would not accept the Dwarf Lords and their weapons. Were these the kinds of people that the Grandiose King created?

As a respected general in the Dwarven army and their chief blacksmith, none of the Dwarves exercised more loyalty than Helimslynch. With all of his loyalty for his fellow Dwarves, however, Helimslynch shared an advanced disdain and distrust for anything or anyone viewed as a threat to his allies. His short stature and laughable countenance made him exactly like his fellow Dwarves. His eagerness and ability in combat made him respected and trusted among his race. For all of the trust that his fellow Dwarves gave Helimslynch, he returned that in full. For all of the abuse that the humans offered Helimslynch, he gladly returned that; with his axe, Warcleaver. Through the unreligious, the Dwarves once understood that they had that opportunity to strike back against the church and their members. However, *ages passed and the human troops siding with the unreligious learned to practice the prejudice to cast aside their Dwarven neighbors as well. Through prejudice, humans, religious and unreligious alike, made dangerous enemies with the fiery tempered, strong, war-minded blacksmiths. Those who dismissed the aid of the Dwarves felt the misfortune of dismissing their weapons and war strategies.*

However, for all of the hatred and mistrust that the Dwarves returned to the humans and Elves, they hated the thought of war even worse. Granted that they were strong, war-minded, and good with weapons, war was just as likely to cost the Dwarves their Dwarven brothers and sisters as cost them their enemies. Helimslynch understood that and doubted that the idea of war was a machination of any human heart. Either way, Helimslynch sensed the hand of a Great Evil over Trina and wasn't so certain whether or not it was the Grandiose King. He just knew that he had to fight it to bottle up the idea of war. Would Helimslynch, for his war-like nature, ability with weapons, and sense of loyalty prove a welcome addition to the Trinity? Or would his suspicion against the church and its teachings prove a hindrance to the Knight of Salvation's cause?

Thunder exploded through the air as lightning erupted from the skies. Whereas Trina's shores appeared enveloped in light, particularly around blessed Dawn Valley, a twilight phantom of misery enveloped the Iron Mountains. Even the arrival of the Knight of Salvation could not penetrate the thick twilight or steer off the weather that served as a reminder of the rage of the Dwarves. Clearly, the atmosphere had not heard of Jovan Bourg, Son of the Church, and was not going out of its way to accommodate him. The sensation was almost refreshing as the Great Evil wouldn't accommodate his arrival either. Behind Jovan, he could hear the grunts and exclamations of exertion from nimble Armin. Clearly, Armin's athleticism was restricted to the treetops and his speed to hilly plains. The jagged rock ridge marking the assent of the Iron Mountains was something else altogether and the bow and blades that he prided himself with so much that he would not leave them with Swift now just got in the way of his travels.

"So, this is where the unlearned Dwarves are cursed to live?" Armin's observation was barely audible beneath the weather. Jovan found the first narrow path devoid of the direct requirement of rock climbing, paused, and hoisted Armin to the narrow path as well.

"This is where the quite *competent* and *resourceful* Dwarves *choose* to live." Jovan announced, "Let us rest a moment before continuing on."

"I meant not to question their intelligence and abilities." Armin insisted, taking a seat on the narrow ledge for a moment while Jovan joined him, "They are unlearned in the spirits of faith because of their bitter stubbornness against listening."

"It might also be observed that they will not listen to religious edicts because of the common practice of casting them aside for the aesthetic consequences of their birth." Jovan concluded, "You forget, as of late, they will not service the unbelieving either."

"But, if they believed," Armin asked, "would they not look more like us? It would be such a blessing as to bring them from their mountain caves to see the world."

"They are born as they are born and not one of us is born believing or not; those are learned practices." Jovan announced, rising from his place and producing a pair of small picks to assist him in what remained of his climb. "Additionally, I would not ask that the Dwarven folk be born to completely resemble their Elf and human neighbors. Let us continue in our quest to seek momentary refuge from such a storm, obtain our new ally, and return to our noble steeds."

It took Armin an extra moment or two to realize what he had just said of the Dwarves right in front of the man destined by Scripture to protect *all* of Trina from the unseen evil that continuously tugged at humanities heartstrings.

"Wait a minute; I didn't mean--." Armin amended; then, upon realizing that he was talking to himself: "Hey, wait for me."

The ascent up the side of Iron Mountain was a treacherous climb. Still, perseverance eventually did prod the appointed Knight of Salvation to the topmost peak where the entrance to the Dwarves' cavern was. However, as Jovan reached the peak, he promptly froze and removed his helmet.

Armin, not too far behind anymore, wondered why Jovan had promptly paused in his climb and graced the mountaintop with his human face. Upon reaching the peak, Armin Kinston realized why and dropped his blades and even his prized bow and quiver of arrows. Standing before the two full-sized young adult males were three short, stocky Dwarves. The Dwarves outnumbered them; and they still had spears and axes aimed at the heroes.

"Hold, friends of Iron Mountain." Jovan requested, casting aside his blade with his helmet, "We have come to petition you on behalf of the Trinity."

Some grumbles and grunts were traded between the Dwarves in a language that was native only to their own kind. Armin could only strain himself to try to understand the conversation of their armed captors. Jovan got the gist of what was being said and nodded in understanding even before one such Dwarf approached the pair.

"This way, Son of Church and Elf!" the Dwarf spat, kicking the pile of weapons to scatter them.

"We come on behalf of the church!" Armin protested as one of the Dwarves brandished a spear at his back.

"Any petition of men can be delivered to full council." The leader of the captors announced, "And any petition of the church shouldn't bother to ring on our hallways."

"Please; we just--." Armin persisted. Still, Jovan raised a hand for silence and obediently began the death march into the cavern at the repeated insistence of the guards. Upon seeing the unarmored, human form of the Knight of Salvation obeying the edicts of a simple group of Dwarves, the captors each shared a puzzled look, then ushered the Elven archer along. As Armin was moved away from his pile of weapons, only to have the items collected by his Dwarven captors, he began his negotiations to get his weapons back. By contrast, Jovan allowed the Dwarves to handle his weapons and armor and silently pleaded Armin to follow suit. The human and Elf were in the other peoples' kingdom; that made them ambassadors and visitors.

The fires of the kiln that composed the core of Iron Mountain seemed intent on burning the prisoners as Jovan and Armin entered. Still, the fire was the only source of welcome light in the cavernous mountain core. Yet, the Dwarves didn't seem all that put off by the heat, the flames, or the darkness that would otherwise engulf them. They were, however, plenty perturbed by the human and Elven prisoner; especially upon recognizing the human as the loudest voice and proudest face of the church. As the two captives continued on their way down the winding paths, several Dwarven blacksmiths glanced up from the fire pit where their weapons resided and the fire of hatred was represented in their eyes. Jovan and Armin hadn't reached their intended destination yet; but they knew that they were in for a long journey.

A huge cavern at the very edge of the core of Iron Mountain was devoid of the pit of fire. It was also the very largest, most comfortable, and best decorated chamber. This unique chamber held the Dwarven high council, thus revealing the fact that not even the Dwarves were above the expression of hierarchy. On the throne in the center of the vaunted head cavern sat Temecar. The high-most Dwarf Lord was surrounded on all sides by his most loyal supporters and honor guard as Jovan and Armin were deposited into the cavern on all fours, deprived of their weapons and armors and covered by their armed escorts. As the heroes remained on all fours, one of their captors barked over them in the native Dwarven tongue to address their ruler. Upon receiving the message, Temecar's face drew into a vicious snarl.

"What edict would the *human* church come to deliver in our halls?" Temecar demanded.

Jovan raised his head from its knelt position enough to speak.

"Temecar, King of Dwarves, my apologies for this intrusion in your hallowed halls of the Iron Mountains." He announced, "We have come with a decree to adopt one of yours into the Great Fellowship to aid me in my quest against the unforeseen evil and to keep me on my course."

"Your Grandiose King extends his religious edicts to the Dwarf Lords of Iron Mountain now?" Temecar demanded, "Is this the same Grandiose

King that your church invokes by name to explain why we are relegated to the halls of Iron Mountains?"

Somehow, Armin had decided that that last remark had been meant for him to answer and lifted his head out of turn.

"My friends, none should have to be relegated only to the Iron Mountains." Armin opined, "If you would only--."

Temecar banged his mighty ceremonial spear for silence.

"Iron Mountain is our *home,* Elf of Arrogance!" Temecar roared, gesturing at the nearest Dwarf, "Noble Helimslynch, take these arrogant idol-worshippers to the dungeon! We Dwarves shall match with this unseen Evil and succeed with or without the church's proposed Knight of Salvation!"

"Hold, Lord Temecar." Jovan persisted, rising back to his feet at the prodding of a spear in his back, "My ally has spoken out of turn. He knew not that you were not speaking in seriousness against Iron Mountain."

Here, the activity in the throne room gave pause as Temecar glowered at the intruder.

"You, a human intruder, would dare to demand my mercy?" Temecar demanded. "Lord of the Church, do you not truly understand what your precious church has done to my people?"

"I did not come here to *demand* anything of the true residents of Iron Mountain." Jovan insisted. "I have only come as the Knight of Salvation to extend an invitation to one of your own to aid me in my quest and keep me on the proper path in this quest. Of late, I also mean to apologize for my friend."

Helimslynch impatiently signaled his soldiers to escort the heroes away to the dungeons for their crimes of speaking out against the Dwarven king. Still, another bang from the ceremonial spear stopped them once more.

"An apology; from a human to a Dwarf?" Temecar grunted, the fire in his auburn eyes dying to suspicion.

"Only in its sincerest form from a guest to his host." Jovan reassured him.

Temecar grumbled to Helimslynch in Dwarven tongue and indicated Jovan.

"You may remain among us for the duration of your time here, Son of the Church." Temecar grunted. "Your weapons, your armor, and your Elf may not. Take the Elvish one; I wish to speak with the human in confidence."

As Armin protested once more, he was promptly escorted from the chamber with much louder protests than before. Jovan took only a moment to wonder what had driven him to select the Elf for his first ally. Then the hero turned back to face Temecar.

"My ally will be treated well?" Jovan asked.

"Your Elven friend will be treated as an Elf!" Temecar spat, "Those steeds reported to be grazing at the foot of our mountain; they are yours?"

"Danavas and Swift; they are ours." Jovan confirmed.

"Then your nonjudgmental *stallions* will be regarded with our greatest care." Temecar reassured him. "You are heralded as a savior for the religious and you have come to Iron Mountain to recruit a Dwarf to your cause; why is this?"

"I am called a Savior for *Trina*; and Trina is equal parts religious and unreligious." Jovan insisted. "The Sacred Text has not scripted for me who represents the Trinity. I have determined that a noble Trinity should be willing to aid me in combating this evil. This Fellowship should represent equal parts believer and unbeliever if only to maintain the interests of *all of* Trina."

Temecar reclined back on his throne and rubbed his many chins in thought. His unkempt, fiery auburn beard concealed anything on his face that would betray his decision before he was ready to profess such a creed and Jovan waited.

"If you are willing to bring your edicts to Iron Mountain, knowing the hospitality that would await you here," Temecar declared, "then you can have the full support of the entire Dwarven army and all of our weapons if you so wish!"

"It is a generous and mighty offer from the Dwarf Lords of Iron Mountain." Jovan pronounced. "But no. I have come here in search of *one*. Helimslynch, noble, loyal, and strong. He has reportedly faced down this Evil before?"

"He and his full unit; nearly beat the rotten thing with no aid from the believer-kind too!" Temecar boasted in the gruff sense of hospitality that the Dwarf Lords were known for. "The church has sent you to uproot our chief general from his home where he is most needed?"

"His aid will be greatly appreciated, King Temecar." Jovan insisted. "The planet Trina will depend on his loyalty and fighting spirit as much as they rely on Armin's bowmanship, swordsmanship, agility, and cunning. I shall return to the church before we set out on this dangerous task and decree that Iron Mountain and its settlers remain under full protection from persecution until the source of this Great Evil can be exorcised from this world."

"To blindly trust our historic persecutors to protect us?" Temecar grunted, "Your *Grandiose King*, if he is more than superstition, is more daft than I thought to have granted you the mantle Knight of Salvation!"

"You have good reason to not trust my word, King Temecar. It will be many years before I can truly believe the decree that *I* am to be the Knight of Salvation myself." Jovan admitted. "The sake of a planet torn asunder for too long by war depends upon the success of this task. The church has determined that the proper reading of Sacred Passages passes the mantle of protector on to me."

"Then when war tears down the churchfolk," Temecar bellowed, "let the Dwarves and unbelievers rebuild in their stead!"

"I'm afraid that war plays no favorites in who gives their lives." Jovan observed. "My petition has fallen upon impatient ears; I pray that my apology will ring on more favorable ones. I shall collect my blade, armor, steed, and, with your permission, the archer. We will take our leave from present company."

"You would take upon yourself the authority to release a prisoner of Iron Mountain?" Temecar demanded. "Such brashness is indeed the understood language of the Dwarf Lords, child! Helimslynch..."

It was the last spoken word that most humans would understand. Helimslynch marched back into the room at his king's beckon call and the two traded private discourse in the ancient Dwarven tongue for several minutes as Jovan remained forgotten. Finally, the conversation was over and Helimslynch regarded Jovan once more. Jovan, for his part, still had to wait for Helimslynch to address him, lest he give away that the sacred Dwarven tongue had fallen on understanding ears...

"This way you will find your Elf and your weapons!" Helimslynch offered, not so much escorting Jovan away as muscling passed him and allowing him to follow. "Your noble beast is well cared for while he stays. Nice looking creature too."

"Thank you." Jovan remarked. "Reports of the offensiveness of Dwarven kind have been greatly exaggerated."

"And reports of the arrogance and stupidity of Elven kind cannot be stressed enough!" Helimslynch barked. "Keep coming; your weapons and your Elf are down this next tunnel."

The pair continued down the tunnels until they both came to a cell nearest the fiery core of Iron Mountain. Resting precariously over the natural kiln furnace were the heroes' weapons and armor. In a dangling cage was Armin Kinston, the archer whose humility was only really celebrated amongst his Elven kin who were more proud than he was. As the new pair passed into the cavern, Armin's heart sank when he saw the unlearned Dwarf first, brandishing his axe; and his hope soared when he saw the Knight of Salvation. Still, to the archer's chagrin, both free men passed the dangling cage and loosed the steeds from a neighboring cavern. Then, to both believers' chagrin, Helimslynch brandished his axe once more and advanced on the fire pit. For the briefest moment, Armin saw his life flash before his eyes in a pit of fire and Jovan really didn't see himself stopping the Dwarf.

Helimslynch took a moment to realize what the others thought he was getting ready to and afforded a gritty chuckle. With precise care, he used his axe to carefully fish the Icarus Blade and glistening white armor away from the flames. Then, with the weapons pulled away from the kiln, his fiery gaze fell on the human Son of the Church.

"If you claim yourself the mantle of Knight of Salvation as you say," Helimslynch grunted, haughtily, "try these on!"

Jovan gingerly accepted the helmet and armor that would conceal his identity and lionize him back to the respected status of Knight of Salvation. The more that he thought about the superficial respect based on human interpretations of the Sacred Text, the more that Jovan hated it. Still, in this instance, the Dwarven general was waiting for him to mask himself and the Elven archer was not scheduled to live forever under the care of the Dwarf Lords. Before the collective gaze of the captured Elf, both of their noble steeds, and their captor, Jovan clamped the armor around his body and placed the helmet over his head. As Helimslynch gaped in an awe not normally expressed by the Dwarves, Jovan Bourg loosed the Icarus from its hilt and placed the ancient heirloom, blade down, in the ground to anchor it in place. Within moments, the molten kiln at the Iron Mountain's core radiated an intense light against the blade. Once more, the simple war weapon and heirloom was elevated to the illusion of a glowing cross. That cross reflected so much promise for the future of Trina that Helimslynch's open-mouthed astonishment betrayed his countenance yet again.

"The Kn-Knight of Salvation is truly the S-Son of the *Church!*" Helimslynch grunted. "Begging your pardon, Majesty of the Cloth; I did not believe before. We of the Iron Mountains do not take a listening ear to the fairytales of your Sacred Text."

"An understandable mistake." Bourg reflected. "The church has for too long misrepresented the teachings of the Sacred Text. However, the words of a Knight of Salvation were true and I mean to assemble a Fellowship. A Great Evil is governing the hearts of man and..."

"I believe that such an Evil does exist." Helimslynch interjected. "But you brought your petition for your Trinity *here*; to the Dwarves?"

"The Dwarves are inhabitants of Trina as well, my little friend." Bourg observed, "And it is recorded in history that they have confronted this evil before. However, this petition has been presented to the Iron Mountains long enough to be viewed as an intrusion. Loose my ally and our steeds and we will take our leave. The Dwarves will know protection from persecution."

"You shall ride from here backed by your Elf, your steeds," Helimslynch grunted, smashing the chain that had levitated the cage and lowering the stunned Armin to safety, "and a Dwarven general and his trusted Warcleaver! While you have not influenced King Temecar's wishes, you have convinced mine. Elvish one, take up your arms and mount your steed. Your quest is continuing with my aid!"

TALIAN

The Celestial Guardians of Seraphic Forest and the mountain of Tress were regarded as descendants of Heaven on a direct line to ascension from the Great Savior. In such cherubic terms, the Guardians were viewed as protectors for the church and for all of its edicts. Believers trusted them; the nonbelievers still respected their powers of flight and magic without explanation. As residents atop the mountain of Tress, some even believed them the personal Guardians or even direct descendants of the Elven line. Still, regardless, of the explanation as to where they came from, they existed and appeared as worshippers.

Among the Guardians resided Princess Talian, a direct descendant of the royal line in all of their beauty, authority, and advanced control over magic. What she did not share with the rest of her royal blood was their sense of self-importance. The lack of a sense of self-importance seemed to reflect right back on what made her attractive and even seemed to increase her powers. After all, of all of the Guardians, it had been Talian who had come the closest to encountering the great evil looming over Trina; and had not only survived the task but had come close to succeeding.

It was an hour so dark that even the Celestial Guardians had almost grown reduced by the dark hatred that enveloped humankind. As suspicion and prejudice loomed even over the Guardians, Talian slipped away under cover of night and used her magic to detect the source of the Evil.

It was nightfall and the world was still at war when a dreaded mist descended from the Heavens. Within moments, the mist enveloped the winged princess and sought to destroy her by suffocation if destroying her by her own hatred had not succeeded. Within moments, Talian could no longer fly under the weight of suffocation and even her magic seemed gone.

It was a long, hard-fought struggle from dusk until dawn as the pains of an otherwise unknown Evil surrounded her. Nevertheless, as her grit and determination allowed her to survive until morning, the beauty of sunrise seemed to burn away some of the Evil's strength. With some of her power restored, a last ditch reserve of magic *dispelled the direct attack. Talian had won. It was a single victory but it was enough to prevent such weakening hatred from overwhelming the Guardians ever again. They could again observe the planet of Trina and do everything in their power to prevent humans from destroying one another. For her efforts Talian was honored as a heroine whose legend would survive generations to come.*

For Talian's ability to confront the Evil directly and win and for her role as majestic observer, she would appear a logical choice to join the Trinity in keeping on the proper path. Still, what does a logical choice mean to the Sacred Text? While it is a human understanding that Talian would contribute to the Trinity, what if there is a darkness on the horizon that could hinder her joining of the quest?

Upon descending Iron Mountain, the newly formed trio marched their heroic steeds through the night and across the desert of Scilia. Their destination was the Seraphic Forest to collect the final member of their troupe. The faithful members of such a troupe rode a brilliant silver and white stallion, a dutiful light brown mare, and one diligent, dung grey mule. The mule, much like its rider, carried an air of enough determination and heart to more than make up for its unsightliness. Still, it wasn't enough for the Elvish Armin.

"The mighty Dwarf and his pack animal, off to rid Trina of evil." Armin chortled from astride noble Swift.

Jovan did all that he could to ignore such ruthless banter. It had, after all, been directed at a fellow member of the Fellowship. Helimslynch was not the type to let such a vulgar remark go unchecked.

"Faithful Bob has carried me on many a journey; and he was at my side once before when I faced the Evil that we seek!" Helimslynch spat in consternation. "How many times has your nag faced down an evil so great, Elf of Prettiness?"

"I am an archer and a hunter, little one." Armin declared.

"And I am a Dwarven *General*!" Helimslynch insisted from near Swift's tail. "If anyone should learn where respect is due, then let such a lesson begin with you!"

The White Knight of Salvation had been too silent for too long as the witty banter had promptly escalated to hateful words.

"Each member of this quest is blessed with many praiseworthy gifts." Jovan announced. "Come; we must proceed toward the mountain community of Tress and the Guardians."

"A mountain community!" Helimslynch barked, "It sounds of a hearty group to reside there!"

"Glorious Heavenly Guardians, friend Helimslynch." Armin amended. "These majestic angels have dwelt amongst the Elven highest castes on the mountains of Tress as protectors for many years. The most blessed of believers call Tress and neighboring Dawn Valley home."

"Bah; more pretty-faced believers!" Helimslynch grunted. "The most blessed of unbelievers will keep the mountain pass of the Iron Mountains as our home!"

"Your kind has much to learn of the Sacred Text to become as enlightened as the faithful Elves, my stout friend." Armin chuckled, navigating Swift forward.

Helimslynch spat at such an idea. It was the Knight of Salvation who had finally heard enough and put his next complaint into words.

"If the unbelievers are to see enlightenment," Jovan observed, "then it is the church who has much to learn in the proper way to teach, most Humble of Dawn Valley. The mountain pass leading to Tress is just ahead, friends."

Carried in their paths by their vigilant steeds, the unlikely heroes pressed forward on the last leg of their journey. Near sunset, they reached the foothills that would lead up the mountainside and into the community of Elves situated atop Tress. Upon arrival, Jovan steered Danavas to one side and anchored his reins to a nearby tree. Danavas, understanding of his master's quest, waited patiently and without a sound of protest. Still, before the horse turned to graze peacefully, he rested his nuzzle on his master's shoulder for good luck. Jovan patted the steed's head in gratitude and began the climb to approach the ruling class of elves once again. This time, his plea was to recruit one of their Celestial Guardians. As Jovan began the simple climb, however, Armin remained rooted in place at Swift's side.

"The ascent of a simple hill is too much for you?" Helimslynch grunted, riding up alongside the Elven rider and his steed.

"The royal Elf Lords of Dawn Valley live atop Tress." Armin observed.

"Royal people willing to pay homage to some Grandiose King for their prettiness!" Helimslynch spat. "Sounds like a nice place for *you* to visit."

"You don't understand, my friend." Armin insisted. "Even I am not welcome on Mount Tress."

"They won't keep your company either, eh?" Helimslynch crowed.

For the first time since the conversation started, Armin turned to face Helimslynch. A dejected look crossed his Plaster-of-Paris, Elven complexion as he recounted his time with the Elves.

"I am royalty by adoption." Armin explained, "Only the lower castes living in Dawn Valley have ever truly accepted me on our shores."

"Then grace your lower caste family with the knowledge of your brief return." Helimslynch grunted with as much sincerity as he had mustered since meeting Armin. "No Dwarf would ever be cast out of their family on such grounds as petty caste differences. Lord Temecar would forbid such an act of disunity."

Armin gazed down upon his stalwart ally once more, widening his eyes in disbelief.

"Temecar exercises such authority over his Dwarves as to oversee how separate family units of Dwarves treat one another?" The Elf asked.

Here, Helimslynch shook his shaggy head.

"No separate family units; one united family of Dwarves, all brothers and sisters together." The Dwarven General scoffed, "You Elvish ones are unfamiliar with such a concept of family?"

Armin flushed red in the face at the question. No, the Elves had never practiced such a simple definition of family.

"Come; while Jovan must confer with the royals and Celestial Guardians," Armin beckoned, "perhaps the lowest castes of my Elven family might be pleased to meet my new Dwarven Brother?"

As Armin moved towards the village of Dawn Valley without his steed, Helimslynch shuddered at the thought presented to him. He then reached into the saddle pouch attached to Swift and removed a small book.

"Bah; so this'd be the Sacred Text that 'Brother' Elf spoke of!"

Helimslynch spat, stuffing the procured book into his mule's saddle sack. "Stay here, Bob. The pretty Elves are expecting company for them to try to 'save' from his ugliness."

The Elven ruling class stood atop Mount Tress, enjoying the view presented before them in Dawn Valley. As King Oran gazed out over the lower castes that he presided over, however, he observed that the lower castes first rose up in celebration over something. It was moments later that shouts of celebration lowered to murmurs of confusion. Oran narrowed his eyes that he might block out his surroundings and see better over great distances. Had the Knight of Salvation returned once more to amend his original mistake of not adopting Kinik or Luciana to his cause? No, the form approaching the lower castes was clearly not the Knight of Salvation. The archer had returned to a kingdom where he had never been truly welcomed and brought a beastly Dwarf with him. Oran signaled for his nearby guards to put an end to any civil unrest due to Armin's return. Still, the guards were no longer available. As Oran whirled around to see what had happened, his noble guards were intercepting the armored form of Jovan.

"Son of the Church, you have returned!" Oran declared, signaling the twins of royalty that they might follow him, "You have recognized your error of taking Armin with you; or perhaps that of the Dwarf that has come to visit our land with him? You wish to adopt Kinik and Luciana to your noble cause?"

"Not this day, King Oran; I am sorry." Jovan announced, "Armin and the Dwarf, Helimslynch, can serve me well to keep me on the righteous path as members of the Fellowship. I do, however, come seeking the aid of one of your Celestial Guardians; the princess, Talian."

Here, King Oran took a step back from the visitor, his demeanor soured.

"You return to our shores to deny Elves of true royal heritage once more, you return an unwelcome addition to Dawn Valley," Oran demanded, "and you have come to deny us one of our celestial protectors?"

"Please understand, your majesty; I do not return here meaning disrespect to your kingdom or your family." Jovan announced, kneeling in the king's presence and dislodging his helmet. "The royal family is needed to remain together as a strong ruling front. As to Armin and Helimslynch, they shall take their leave when I do."

All was silent for a moment; followed by the flapping of wings and the arrival of several shadowy figures. The new figures were humanoid in build but each bore a pair of wings and iron masks to conceal their faces. A select group of Guardians had arrived.

"The Son of the Church and the church itself are no longer any friends of the Elven Lords." Oran announced. "Take the Knight of Salvation and his followers from my presence and deliver our new decree to the church. They have made a powerful batch of enemies."

As Jovan craned his neck around, he found himself surrounded on all sides by Guardians, each bearing a staff. Naturally, the Icarus Blade could have gotten the White Knight of Salvation out of his latest predicament but...no. He had not come to fight with the Guardians. He had not even come with the intent to offend the Elven Lords. However, his renewed intention required their king to listen to reason. Jovan nodded his understanding of the king's wishes and the Guardians backed away a few steps but stayed nearby in case of a trick.

"Take the Fellowship that you have already gathered and take your leave." Oran instructed once more, "You have heard the will of the Elf Lords of Dawn Valley."

"I understand." Jovan announced, approaching the edge of the mountain of Tress, "Friends, remount your steeds that we may leave. We will have to search for our new ally elsewhere."

Armin had overheard the heated exchange atop the mountain, realized that most of what had been said was because of him, and was crestfallen once more. Years of being ostracized from his adopted royal family had reached the fruition of punishing those around the archer. He approached the foot of Mount Tress and fell to one knee as would a member of the lower caste.

"Father," Armin declared as he dislodged his bow and quiver of arrows and rested his swords on the ground, "I surrender my bow, my swords, and my place on this quest over to Kinik and Luciana. Noble Knight of Salvation, you would do well on this quest against an unnecessary Evil by accepting Kinik, Luciana, and noble Helimslynch to guide you in a righteous path."

Oran narrowed his eyes sharply once more, his blue-silver eyes cutting sharply through the archer who he would never call "son."

"No *true* son or daughter of mine will ever mount up alongside a heathen Dwarf!" Oran spat. Behind the king, the prince and princess clearly agreed with the declaration amidst folded arms and matching looks of venom.

For as narrow as the views of the ruling class were, a rallying cry came from the lower castes of Elven Lords assembled within Dawn Valley and intent on welcoming their celebrated, most humble archer home.

"Take up your weapons; *you* are the one who deserves to ride for the Fellowship."

"Your bow and this Dwarf's axe will ring true against any evil!"

"Hail the assembled Fellowship!"

"**This** is the will of **these** Elf Lords of Dawn Valley, Majesty."

Amidst the cries of support, the prince and princess exchanged looks of clear shock and disappeared back into their palace that they might no longer face down the people that they presided over. Oran's lips drew themselves into a thin line and he turned back to face the Knight of Salvation once more, his back once again to the people that he had ruled for so many years.

"If this be the true will of the Elf Lords," Oran boomed, "take the archer and your Dwarf once more. May the Great Almighty speed *you*, Knight of Salvation, on your quest. Talian, the majestic beauty, is in Seraphic Forest at present. My Guardians may bring her here to you."

"You have been more than accommodating for our stay, King of Elves." Jovan announced, "If one of the Guardians might only lead the way to Seraphic Forest that we might approach Talian personally, we will not trouble you or your people again. I only pray for the day when you will rejoin your unity with the church, regardless of this fateful visit from but one representative."

Oran nodded briskly and snapped his fingers to signal a single Guardian.

"Here is your guide; take your leave, Son of Church." Oran murmured, "I should pray that your church will be happy to host the archer upon your successful return."

The meaning was clear. Jovan, the Son of the Church, had no business returning to Dawn Valley; and with good cause. Years of learned prejudice prevented Helimslynch from being welcomed on Dawn Valley's shores; that was understood. Now Armin, heralded as a champion of humility by the lower castes, was cast out of his home realm by royal decree. The Elves pledged much gratitude toward a Great Almighty that had crafted their aesthetic beauty. There remained many lessons to learn about *true* worship. Jovan left the elves to learn their lessons and fetched the steeds.

The voyage from Dawn Valley to Seraphic Forest passed in silence. Jovan continued to lead the expedition in a sense of silence and the gathered members of the Fellowship had nothing to say to one another pending what had happened at Dawn Valley. When things had been quiet for long enough, Helimslynch decided that he had something to say.

"I'd have never believed it." the Dwarf grunted. "With the Elven folk, *you* truly are the most humble."

"I can hardly believe it myself, little friend." Armin replied, steering Swift forward without ever looking back to reveal his crestfallen demeanor to his new ally.

"Worry not, Armin." Jovan added, "For your aid as a member of this Fellowship, the White Knight of Salvation and Son of the Church will guarantee that you will always have a home in the church. Friend Helimslynch, you and your Dwarven brothers will always be protected from persecution and prejudice so long as a Knight of Salvation walks Trina."

From high above the heroes, Flyte, their winged guide, indicated the Seraphic Forest just ahead of the expedition.

"Through there you'll find Princess Talian." Flyte announced, flapping his brilliant white wings. Though a ceremonial mask concealed the expression of Flyte's true face, he sounded embittered. It either represented the fact that he had never been summoned to the expedition, that the Elves that Flyte protected had been so recently offended, or that the expedition was taking his princess. Either way, the winged Guardian had taken the heroes as far as he was willing and promptly turned away to head back to Mount Tress. As the Guardian flew away, Helimslynch narrowed his eyes at the retreating form.

"Hmph, your deity-sent Guardians aren't a very friendly bunch." the Dwarf spat.

"We have offended the Elf Lords that he swore to protect and are conspiring to adopt his princess to our cause." Armin explained. "Though, to get her to agree might present a problem as well, White Knight."

"The Fellowship won't adopt anyone against their will." Jovan vowed, "But we can do no harm in asking. Come, allies, through that clearing."

With that, the heroes pressed forward and into the clearing. What they hadn't seen behind them were the two Guardians monitoring their approach. Those same Guardians emerged from the treetops to signal the Iron Vines to block the heroes on their path without escape. Not one member of the Fellowship knew that they were blocked in on their path and both winged guardsmen fled by the treetops to alert their king to the sudden arrival of intruders.

Twilight was beginning to settle over all of Trina and not even the ethereal beauty of Seraphic Forest could protect the riders from the weight of dusk on their war torn home world. Helimslynch took in the descending sense of the surrounding sunset as darkness settled over Trina and took it upon himself to liven up the mood of the expedition.

"Hey, Archer!" he grunted. "Bob and I haven't eaten our fill for two days expedition; and the fruit in those trees looks satisfying!"

The tree didn't have to be specified, nor did the fruit. Armin's Elven eyes had spotted the tasty morsels from a mile away and identified them as the most succulent. His means of receiving the luscious treats for his stout companion didn't need to be specified either. The request was a test and it was a test that not even the most humble among Elves could resist putting to rest. He reached into his quiver and selected a single arrow. With that, he lifted his bow from the saddle sack without ever realizing that his copy of the Sacred Text was gone, loaded the arrow, squinted for optimal vision, and let fly with the projectile. The projectile pierced the smallest portion of the bushel of fruit without damaging any of the treats and six pieces of fruit tumbled toward the earth and right into Swift's saddle sack. Six pieces of fruit from a full bushel now rested in the expedition's possession, the rest of the tree was unharmed, and, save for Helimslynch's impressed grin or the stern glare from Jovan Bourg, no one really had to be the wiser.

With barely a whisper of wings against air, however, Armin was proven mistaken in his original speculation and certainly in his earlier actions. Within moments of flying low enough that his wings had made any disturbance of noise, a single Guardian clipped Armin from Swift's saddle to the steed's fruitless protests. Another Guardian swooped in on Helimslynch and a third grabbed Jovan from their startled steeds. The Holy Fellowship had intruded in someone else's land and were thieves besides. They now had to await punishment for both crimes at the mercies of their captors.

The following morning, sunrise burned its way into Jovan's subconscious, announcing that a night's rest had separated twilight from daybreak. The fact that the sun was rather intense in his eyes told the Knight of Salvation that his helmet was gone. The sight of the armed winged guards, no horses, and the binding of Iron Vines reminded Jovan why they were still in Seraphic Forest. Surrounding Jovan, Armin gazed longingly along the way at his bow, quiver of arrows, and swords until his eyes shut once more. Helimslynch, however, had just been awakened by the sudden sunlight as well and was now using his renewed vigor to struggle against the Iron Vines, snarling and spitting as he did so.

Time passed and the heroes were still in their natural restraints. However, at a moment's notice, the Guardians suddenly backed away respectfully. It was only a few moments before their captives knew why. Amidst the Celestial Guardians, their faces concealed by iron masks, a new form arrived. This new arrival wore not a mask but a ceremonial helmet that revealed his face. More importantly, however, he commanded the respect of even the Celestial Guardians. King Stratus, their lord and Princess Talian's father, had arrived on the scene having heard about the "thievery" from the intruders and was none too happy.

"These are the ones who thought to intrude in our forest and plunder from and damage our fruit trees?" Stratus Arrack demanded.

Armin, the offending archer in question, opened his mouth to explain but one of the arresting guards beat him to it.

"Yes, my lord." The guard replied. "I captured the archer myself; and I present you with the bow and quiver of arrows that he meant to use."

Stratus seized the bow and quiver of arrows for closer inspection, sniffed as if trying to pick up the scent on the bow, and glowered at the Elf.

"The most celebrated of Elven archers would dare to trespass here and damage our crops?" Stratus demanded, raising a golden trident.

"King Stratus, this is a misunderstanding." Jovan explained, "Our expedition simply..."

"I did not permit you to speak in my presence!" Stratus barked, "Archer?"

"To steal of your fruit tree was a mistake." Armin conceded, "But the remainder of the crop remains undamaged. We represent the Holy Fellowship against the Great Evil that settled upon our shores and we seek the hand and expertise of your princess, Talian..."

"A Dwarf and an Elf represent the Fellowship banking on Trina's survival?" Stratus grunted; then turning to face Jovan, "And *you* are our proposed *Knight of Salvation*?"

Jovan silenced his struggles against the Iron Vines as Stratus approached. As the Guardian paused inches away from the boy's face, however, he gave pause and narrowed his eyes to see the face before him clearer.

"Jovan Bourg, the Son of the Cloth!" Stratus declared, directing a sweeping gesture that caused the Iron Vines binding Bourg to release and retract.

"Yes, Lord Stratus." Bourg confirmed, collapsing freely to one knee before the ruler of another nation. "I humbly apologize for the misunderstanding caused by my party. We did come into your land on terms of peace to entrust your daughter as a member of our movement."

All was silent for a moment; then Bourg felt a hand reaching for the hilt concealing the sword. Instinctively, Bourg went to grapple at a thief; then his eyes met Stratus's as the king of winged people admired the captured weapon.

"If this is truly the Icarus," Stratus addressed his followers, "then the Son of the Church is truly the White Knight of Salvation that precious Trina has sought for so long."

Another sweeping, majestic gesture caused the ground to separate as a rotting stump rose into place. Without so much as a word of command, Stratus inserted the sharp edge of the Icarus into the stump and secured the sword as the other guards backed away. With the blade secured in place, one of the guards performed the third and final gesture. Within moments, the wind picked up and the treetops of the Seraphic Forest separated in the breeze long enough to let in the sunlight. Within moments, the sunlight reflected off of the blade and revealed a glorious, radiant cross in the middle of the Seraphic Forest.

"Truly, they are the Fellowship united by the Great Savior!" Stratus observed, beckoning forth a single Guardian. "Free them and summon the princess. It would do them well for their quest to beobserved by one of our own and one who once drove off the Evil enveloping our land."

The guard nodded his head in understanding. With a sweeping gesture, what remained of the Iron Vine trap cleared away, releasing the accompanying members of the Fellowship back to their freedom. The masked guard then presented the archer's weapons back to him, announcing the fact that he had been the same guard who had caught Armin in the act of thievery before. Finally, the guard revealed the most dramatic surprise of all; *he* relinquished the masked helmet to reveal a *she*. Furthermore, her beauty was of such radiance that even her fellow Guardians paid their respects; yet, she had kept her face hidden beneath a mask similar to those of the other Guardians. Finally, she fastened a silver tiara to the top of her head to hold back her golden curls. There was no question about it; this Guardian was Princess Talian.

"Restore your armors and your mounts." Talian decreed, collecting a nearby staff and tether whip as a golden horned, snowy falcon landed obediently on her shoulder, "I can still sense the source of this Evil on Trina. It is powerful and we have much ground to cover."

With another gesture from her hand, Talian cleared away the Iron Vines that had once blocked the heroes in. A once hidden grave plot appeared on the untouched land.

"A gravesite?" Bourg asked, replacing his armor.

"Investigate, Knight of Salvation." Talian offered, "Dwarf, Elf, perhaps if the two of you could fill a kindly Princess in on our mission..."

Helimslynch followed Talian begrudgingly back to the steeds as Armin followed in a nearly hypnotized state. Alone, Jovan did as advised and stumbled onto the grave plot. It only took the Knight of Salvation a moment to realize that only one grave marker had an inscription. That inscription read **"Maxim Bourg: Father of the Church; Soldier for Society."** He was the one man who could most properly represent both sides of the Great War; and he was the Knight of Salvation's long lost father. Bourg removed his helmet and cemented the Icarus into the ground, then knelt down as he had never done before. Tears threatened his eyes as he turned a silent petition toward the one man who had ever taught him the most in how to properly live his life:

> **Father, the days are coming for me to raise to Trina a blade of righteous justice that the people of Trina, behind this Fellowship's efforts, shall unite as believers and unbelievers to reign and prosper. Guide my strength to execute judgment and righteousness in this new age on Trina.[1]**

EPILOGUE

Martilla Bourg was none too pleased with her son's latest written petition regarding the Dwarves of Iron Mountain. The church was honor bound to respect the Son of the Church's edicts so long as he acted as the Knight of Salvation; however, the ungrateful, unlearned knew no such honor and could not be bound by it. Henceforth, because one Dwarf was a member of the Trinity, the church could not minister to the thuggish brutes. The Dwarves, however, could attack as they pleased.

On one such evening following her son's departure and between his latest written petition and safe return, Joto and Martilla were no longer watching over the family mansion and farm but over the church walls. Even on the very evening that she was delivering her most important edict to her Great King- that he guide the church and guide and protect her son- Joto interrupted with such urgency that the church Elder could not upbraid the rudeness of the offense.

"Mother Superior, Lady of the Church!" Joto cried, "Forgive my brash intrusion during your personal reflection but…"

"My son, the Knight of Salvation; is it news of his return?" Martilla asked.

The very first brick to smash the plate glass ceremonial window announced a piece of news of a different variety. The smashed window was soon answered by shouts of rebellion against the house of worship and its edicts. Mother Superior glanced out the broken window and spied the united front of thuggish unbelievers with Darath Noar leading the way. The soldiers carried swords and bayonets. Furthermore, they were already burning several copies of the Sacred Text, gifted to each of them by the church's missionary soldiers.

"Step forth, Lady of the Church!" Darath, the elected leading voice of rebellion, barked. "We wish to impress upon you what your teachings have truly done to us!"

Martilla Bourg exchanged a long look with Joto. The allies of the church had pooled all of their resources to bring enlightenment to the uneducated. It was the ungrateful heathens representing the unbelieving caste that had smashed the church on this visit and attacked the poor, beleaguered worshippers. As is, the unbelievers were too unwashed and unlearned to understand what the church offered them. There was but one resource that the soldiers of the unbelievers would understand.

"Alert Viscar Halas." Bourg announced, "Tell our missionaries to stand at the ready for the church's first edict."

"Mother Superior, this is a declaration of WAR!" Joto warned.

"It is what the unbelievers understand; and you have heard your Mother Superior." Bourg replied...

FALL OF EVIL

PROLOGUE

Extending across generations, an unseen Evil enveloped beauteous Trina's shores in its attempts to govern the human heart. Approaching unseen allowed such intrusion to go unchecked. Though invisible, however, this ultimate Evil travelled with a great power reflected through the suspicion, anger, hatred, and prejudice resonating from the heart of humanity.

Gorrenwrath, the unseen Evil force, first approached the world of Trina on the tail of a raging tempest. As the storm and darkness settled over the Holy planet of Trina, a darkness settled over the hearts of its inhabitants; a darkness that not even the high religious could overcome alone. Acting invisibly, the darkness navigated the human heart toward unyielding prejudice and suspicion. Such was the Evil dividing Trina's people and silently prompting the world's downfall in warfare.

Only Maxim Bourg, wed to the cloth, a soldier of the unbelievers, and loyal to both, had ever come close to recognizing the Evil and certainly the closest of any mortal to driving it off. Instead, the faithful soldier regretfully died in his attempt and the Holy War of Ages continued unprecedented between a failed church and their lost flock. In Maxim Bourg's absence, there remained only the boy that he had dutifully and faithfully raised to truly appreciate the social justice teachings of the church. That boy, the son of the Mother of the Church and Soldier of the unbelievers, would one day rise to the challenge of becoming the predestined White Knight of Salvation that Trina had waited for for so long to end the war.

*As the tale of the Knight of Salvation unfolded, he united alongside the Trinity to guide him on his quest and wielded the untapped power of the Icarus Blade. However, Gorrenwrath not only utilized his own seemingly unlimited potential but the powers of seven evil servants of his own; disciples of notorious **Greed** (Rumios). **Gluttony** (Daz), **Sloth** (Silax), **Envy** (Mynos), **Wrath** (Drax), **Pride** (Demetrius), and **Lust** (Milana). As Gorrenwrath's wretched adherents, his servants worked in darkness to turn the hearts of the unsuspecting toward sinister temptation. And where they might fail, Gorrenwrath could still succeed as the true source of each of their individual powers.*

As war continued to threaten the weak bonds between believers and unbelievers, Gorrenwrath gathered greater power with every passing day of the war of generations. In due course, Jovan Bourg and his mighty Fellowship gathered more courage in their quest as they constantly gathered more support. The dark ages of war-torn Trina were set to make a change; either to a time of peace with the Knight of Salvation's victory or of certain destruction through a victory for Gorrenwrath's cause. Only time, the success of the Fellowship, and the resilience of the hearts of mammon would determine how the historic War of Ages ended and Trina's survival in generations to come.

GREED

Jovan Bourg was the son of a minister of high authority and of a respected soldier of the unreligious. That naturally made him important. His position of importance as a Son of the Cloth was all that he could understand from his mother's teachings. As to his father's teachings--well, he was unlearned and knew nothing of the proper decorum for one raised in the faith. Jovan Bourg deserved every slice of good fortune that life had to offer him. First of all, the Sacred Text was translated as such; secondly, his mother told him that it was translated as such.

Due to a life of shelter inside of the church walls and amongst all believers save for his rebellious father, Jovan Bourg knew nothing of the outside world until a fateful night that Maxim Bourg had determined that his son would experience life on the outside. In broad daylight and under the cover of a makeshift cleric disguise, Maxim Bourg accessed the church's nursery and stole three-year-old Jovan right passed the watchful eye of faithful Joto. It would be Jovan's first experience in the outside world as his father took him on a trip to the local agricultural market in Krill's square.

Jovan's youthful eyes recorded his surroundings. This was the world outside of the church where the sights and sounds he experienced were not predetermined by his mother as stressed by the Sacred Text!

As his father determined that they were both hungry, he dutifully escorted his young charge to the nearest peddler and ordered his finest loaf. The only other person in line with them was a young girl perhaps twice Jovan's age who clearly could not afford the loaves that this man was peddling. Was she one of the unlearned?

As Jovan recorded the girl with widened eyes of rapt interest, the peddler passed the loaf to Maxim Bourg. Then, in one rapid motion and before Jovan's eyes of bewilderment, the ragged girl swiped the loaf of bread from his father's hands and ran off. She was a thief; one of the unlearned that Jovan had been warned of!

"Father, that unbeliever; she stole our food!" Jovan declared in case his father had missed it and hoping that the nearby soldiers in the market that day heard of the offense against the Son of the Church.

Within moments, a firm hand settled over the boy's mouth.

"Hush, child!" Maxim upbraided the boy as he used his free hand to pay for and collect three juices. With that, Bourg marched the bewildered young Jovan away from the peddler and down a back alley until they rediscovered the young thief. The thief lowered the loaf that was inches away from her first bite, her eyes reflecting fear. Still, Maxim Bourg had another lesson in mind that day. The soldier promptly removed a knife from his satchel and slashed 1/3 of the loaf away, taking the small portion of a loaf of bread that he had bought with his own money for his son and him and leaving the struggling girl a drink besides. As Jovan was ushered away to gnaw his partition of their portion, he did not yet realize what he had just learned.

The seaside village of Callistra was home to many Elves and humans living together in harmony in their glorious village ordained and set aside as a fishing community. War never found Callistra as the rebellious unbelievers and their heathen Dwarvish followers rarely graced Callistra's shores. Even when they did come, the ethereal tranquility governing the seaside village overtook them and no warfare interfered with village life. Only the Callistra Sea graced the village with its ethereal presence.

The Callistra Sea, normally beautiful and peaceful, enveloped the land under cover of night one fateful night. The waters did not strike anyone's home or land to bring destruction to any people. However, they unnaturally undercut the bank of the beach and greedily gulped up the sands. The land nearest the Callistra Sea was clearly its own to take. Voraciously, the seas undercut and gobbled up the land nearest the shore. The villagers murmured something about the anomalies and moved their crops to higher ground before they could be taken. Still, they gave the peculiarities little more thought as the sea never reached their homes.

As the villagers slept the night of the incongruities in the sea's behavior, enough sand and stone was cut away from the land to form what appeared to be a human body. Within moments, the covetous Callistra Sea silenced itself once more. Still, the sweetest sea breeze caused flesh and cloth to form over the sand and stone sculpture. A second burst of sea breeze swept through and the "human body" of sand and stone rose to the occasion.

"Lord Gorrenwrath, your lowly servant, Rumios, hears you and awakens." The lanky, aging construct announced in a high pitched whine beneath stringy raven locks and black cloth. "I will, however, require great power to do your bidding."

A crash of thunder sounded in the great distance without ever disturbing the Callistra Sea again. No other change was noted in the atmosphere. However, the sly grin noting Rumios's face spoke volumes.

"Yes, yes, my lord; that will be more than adequate to bring the demise of the Fellowship." Rumios announced, "When my task is complete, I may collect enough power to rule over Callistra? It was our bargain."

An angry crack of thunder penetrated the atmosphere, disturbing the Callistra Sea back to rage. Rumios merely cackled that he had fueled his master's ire and set out on his way.

As dusk turned to dawn in the Seraphic Forest, Armin determined that the Fellowship had been still for too long. Helimslynch had since gone to sleep. Armin was trying to piece together a conversation with Talian to the best of his abilities. Jovan Bourg remained dutifully knelt alongside the headstone, his helmet removed in respect and his sword anchored to the ground once more where the sun emitted a giant glowing cross. Talian, in turn, waited patiently for the expedition to continue. The winged princess did not seem to mind the delay. However, she deserved to know that at least one man was strong enough to take the role of leadership upon himself. Besides, the great, invisible source of Evil wasn't wasting the same time as the quest to oppose it; nor was it driving itself off in their absence.

"Lady Talian," Armin declared, approaching the Guardian with a sense of timidity that betrayed his business-like voice, "it is time that we leave. The Great Evil settling over our shores and the human condition is not getting weaker as we wait and…"

"We will wait as the White Knight of Trina's Salvation pays his due respects, beautifully handsome one." Talian insisted as the snowy white falcon with golden horns rejoined the proceedings and settled on the winged princess's shoulder.

There it had been; Armin's attempt at a first impression and he had been upbraided for impatience and dismissed as a man of Elven glamour. The archer respectfully rested his glorious bow on the ground and sat down patiently beside it.

Jovan had heard the exchange behind him and knew that, as the Fellowship's leader, he was keeping them from their quest. However, he would not allow this time to be disturbed. The Knight of Salvation had more to say.

In the coming days, I will allow for Trina to be saved
And her people may dwell safely.[2]

Jovan Bourg, the White Knight of Salvation, had spoken his peace to the audience responsible for raising him in any sense of the humility so important in any human relations. He rose back to his feet and collected his helmet and the Icarus before remounting Damascus.

"Thank you, faithful Talian." Bourg said to the woman; then, to each member of the Fellowship, "Mount up, friends. We continue on this quest of nobility."

The voyage left the Seraphic Forest and pressed forward on their journey against the evil that was Gorrenwrath. The three heroes left by way of their steeds and Talian did all that she could to slow her flight that the rest of the expedition might not get separated. From her place in the air, Talian's hands began glowing with mystic energy as if to trace the nearest source of nearby magic. Finally, the winged princess opted to speak.

"Gorrenwrath always arrives on the tail of a storm." Talian announced. "A storm graced the village of Callistra one night past. It has since settled over the desert of Scilia."

"Onward to the desert of Scilia then, friends." Jovan announced, pressing Danavas toward the crossroads separating the Iron Mountains from the mountain of Tress. As the heroes pressed onward, Helimslynch fished a book out of his steed's saddle sack and began chuckling as he read.

"Brother Elf," Helimslynch grunted, "have you ever read to 'keep your treasures close at hand'?"

"Why, yes, of course, my Dwarven Brother." Armin replied, fishing through Swift's saddle sack passed his extra arrows, "It's written to guard the treasures of the heart; it's right here in— "

"The celebrated Sacred Text of your Grandiose King?" Helimslynch demanded with a toothy grin, "Just remember, 'true knowledge comes with SHARING of the Sacred Text'."

"It means to speak of what we have read and share its meaning with those around us; and it does not speak kindly of *thieves*." Armin mused, "Kindly return the book to its rightful owner."

"Bah; and what does your Sacred Text say of FALSE worship?" Helimslynch challenged.

Armin reared up in Swift's saddle at the sound of the indirect charge.

"What do you speak of, Dwarven one?" he contended, the true re-sponse to the charge evident in his voice.

"You claim a 'Great Almighty' but you reserve worship for your own mold and talents." Helimslynch chortled.

"Enough, the both of you." Jovan interjected. "If you are to represent the Holy Trinity if only to keep me on the right path, then I feel it best that we each learn to work as one."

Armin had more to say to the Dwarf on the matter of what had just been said of the Elven race. Still, Helimslynch begrudgingly placed the copy of the Sacred Text back in Swift's saddle sack with a grumbled apology. High above the goings on, Talian arched her eyebrows beneath her masked helmet at the banter between the Elf and Dwarf. Were these the other members of the great Trinity that the Sacred Text had spoken of? Clearly, the White Knight of Salvation had some of his own concerns regarding judgment to contend with. With such a lax of judgment in selecting the members of his own Fellowship, was the Knight of Salvation truly prepared to face the Great Evil that Gorrenwrath represented?

The sands tore about the deserts of Scilia on winds of destruction, scattering the land in its path. Amidst the raging winds, only one life form wandered aimlessly. It was the form of a lanky, pasty, pathetic shepherd with scraggly, shoulder length dark hair and a moth eaten shepherd's crook wandering aimlessly through the desert. As the expedition pressed on their path, the disheveled shepherd raised his eyes in hope. Lo and behold, the lowly shepherd saw the armored rider sitting tall in the saddle of the armored silver and white steed first and foremost. For the briefest moment, the shepherd's skeletal face twisted into a cunning grin as the sandstorm surrounding him picked up in intensity for but a moment.

As the expedition surged forward right into the eye of the unnatural weather patterns in their tireless quest against Gorrenwrath, it was Armin's eyes that penetrated the sandstorm just ahead of them enough to make out a human form.

"A disheveled shepherd." Armin announced, pointing just ahead, "The storm seems to have gathered around him. It must be Gorrenwrath."

"Then the man needs our help," Helimslynch declared, "and this Mister Gorrenwrath needs to meet WarCleaver!"

Jovan drew a glistening boot into Danavas's side and the mighty stallion surged toward the stumbling form of the shepherd. The victim of the storm struggled to shield his eyes from the raging sands as the armored rider approached. Still, he could see nothing.

"Who is it who descends his mounted form on a lowly shepherd?" Rumios demanded, settling a hand on his nearby staff (disguised as a shepherd's crook as he knew the answer), "If you be thieves, then..."

"Holy riders of Trina, friend." Jovan reassured him.

"Then, those behind you; they are the Trinity, the noble Fellowship?" Rumios asked; then, gazing upon the armored knight, "And *you*; you are the most glorious White Knight of Salvation?"

"Jovan, Son of the Church, at the service of the planet Trina and all of her people in need." Jovan announced, "Does our weary traveler friend have a name?"

"Rumios, Shepherd of Callistra." Rumios returned the introduction, "I fear that I have lost my flock in this storm."

"It is fortuitous that the storm did not claim you as well." Armin announced, marching Swift forward and into position, "It is believed by our most noble sorceress that the sandstorm may have been one of wicked Gorrenwrath's many disguises."

"Gorrenwrath, the all-powerful Evil that tampers with the human heart and plagues it toward the self-destruction of war?" Rumios supplied as Helimslynch joined the proceedings and Talian landed alongside Armin, "He is but a legend, isn't he?"

"Well, if he's no fairytale now, he'll wish he were after he meets my WarCleaver!" Helimslynch grunted, slinging his axe.

"I do not believe Gorrenwrath to be a falsehood." Talian announced, "I have once contended with a Great Evil long enough to drive it off for another day. Furthermore, my powers did sense something familiar just now."

"Come, weary traveler." Jovan insisted, "We shall pitch camp for the night and return you to Callistra by dawn. Perhaps your loyal flock will be there waiting for you."

"Many ballads will be written of your kindness, Great Knight; thank you." Rumios gushed. With that, the weathered shepherd mounted Danavas behind Jovan and joined the Fellowship on their latest expedition.

As night graced the planet Trina, darkness enveloped the desert sands of Scilia. Beneath the desert moon, the Fellowship slept as Rumios tended to a dying campfire as he had agreed to do in gratitude. As Rumios gazed over the campfire his, eyes reflected a sense of darkness that seemed to starve for power. He was not as alone as the physical world would seem apparent.

"The Fellowship may not be close with one another but the Trinity holds the Knight of Salvation in highest regard." Rumios hissed, staring into the oncoming darkness. "They will continue to do all that they can to keep him on the path of righteousness. I might dispose of the Fellowship and then crush the Knight himself, but I will require more power to do as you ask."

The campfire that had been dying down to embers roared to life in a brief inferno of rage. Beneath the burning glow, Rumios reflexively shielded his eyes and backed away from the blaze.

"Alright; no more power until the job is done." Rumios conceded, "Fear not. I have already clouded the good Knight's judgment that he has viewed me as a token to perform a selfless deed. It will not be long before I manipulate the sense of greed in him that is truly the birthmark of all humanity, my liege."

As the last embers of the campfire died away, Rumios sensed that sunup was near. It would be mere moments before the archer's attuned Elven senses would recognize the coming of the dawn. Rumios had to act fast if only to put his next plan into motion. Within moments, his mystic staff began glowing from beneath its disguise as a shepherd's crook. A single serpentine beam of energy emerged from the staff's tip. As it struck ground, that serpentine beam of mystic energy adopted skin, fangs, the breath of life, and an evil sense of duty. The dark disciple of greed's magic had given rise to an enchanted cobra, its fangs dripping with venom and its eyes radiating hunger.

"You know what to do at sunup, my putrid pet." Rumios informed the cobra. The cobra answered its master with a rhythmic jutting of its ink black, forked tongue and eyes that radiated at least as much evil as the magic that had created it.

Just like all creatures of Elven birth, Armin sensed the arrival of the dawn from a dead sleep. As the dawn's earliest rays flooded over Trina, Armin's eyes fluttered open and the Elf rose to greet the day as the first member of the Fellowship to awaken. The archer then seized up his bow and quiver from beside him and adjusted the swords at his sides. This had once been the moment when he would reflect on life under his conflict-ing roles as the palace outcast and town hero. However, this morning's concerns were even more ridiculous than usual. Armin's eyes wandered toward the resting form of Talian, wrapped in her own feathered arms as a natural blanket. Armin tried to let his mind wander away from the musings but he did not have the best practice in ignoring the musings of the heart.

Suddenly, if Armin's eyes were fixated on Talian, his Elven ears were tuned to the sounds of the violent hissing behind him. With rapid motions that any other warrior could only help to fathom, Armin load three arrows into his bow. His weapon loaded, the archer used his natural agility and speed to suddenly turn in the direction of the source of the sound. Lo and behold, there stood the disheveled shepherd, still without his flock and using his cane to fend back as well as he could against an advancing cobra. As the cobra arced up on its tail, Armin could clearly see that its fangs dripped with venom, its eyes radiated death, and its body looked capable of crushing the cane to splinters without a second thought. It was anyone's guess what the vicious cobra could have done to the shepherd with no extra effort.

Armin had to act fast on behalf of the suddenly petrified shepherd. Luckily, as an archer and a swordsman who had learned his survival skills from life in the village, he could act faster than most. No sooner were the arrows loaded and he was facing the threat than all three arrows soared forward simultaneously.

Upon spying the unhinged arrows, Rumios leapt back in shock. Seeing its prey leap backward, the cobra prepped itself to lunge and strike. Still, within moments, the three unhinged arrows ended up right where the cobra's prey would have originally been; thereby not harming either living creature but placing a barrier in between them. Startled, the cobra angrily moved to weave its way around the barrier as Armin loaded up a single arrow in lieu of the original three. The first three had been to create the barricade; this one was clearly meant to do more if the cobra didn't give up on its victim and slither away.

Rumios continued trying to mentally control his magic creation long enough for Jovan to awaken and aid him in his fight. Still, the effort would be for naught if the cobra were "killed" by a direct strike from the last loaded arrow. No; the disciple of greed needed to do more to bide his time long enough for Jovan to become involved and be lavished with the credit. Then, Rumios's eyes settled on Talian as the winged enchantress began stirring in her sleep, her mind quietly attuned to the sunlight breaking a new day and the excitement surrounding her. As Rumios focused on the Guardian with a sly grin, his eyes flashed crimson for but a moment. In that moment, the cobra's eyes met his own and they too glowed crimson. The mystic cobra knew what to do.

Rumios lashed at the snake warningly with his cane once more. Promptly, the cobra whipped around, aggravated by the direct hit. As the cobra focused on the direct hit, its eyes settled on Talian's sleeping form in his renewed anger and the cobra lunged. Suddenly, the archer forgot all about his desire to protect life and in his renewed vigor, the archer whipped around and was aiming at the cobra once more.

What happened next took a single moment. A titanium boot stomped on the ground with sufficient force that the cobra was launched airborne, only to land on its side a few feet away and squirm in the blind rage of its confusion.

It had been the crash of the boot that had roused Helimslynch from his slumber like a beckon call to action. Within moments, the stalwart Dwarf wriggled out of his sleeping bag and grabbed WarCleaver.

"Heh; where's...?" Helimslynch demanded, groggily.

"The giant axe won't be necessary, friend." Jovan announced, approaching the struggling cobra and scooping it up into the palm of his gauntlet where it promptly flattened out into a javelin. "Poisonous snakes don't really faze a man in several tons of glistening titanium armor plating."

Jovan drew back his throwing arm and promptly let fly with the startled cobra, hurdling it into the distance where it could land safely beyond the reach where it could harm anyone. The members of the Fellowship all watched in awe as the cobra vanished from sight altogether. No one saw the peculiar glow surrounding Rumios's staff; or the fact that the cobra had not so much vanished over the horizon. Rather, the cobra secretly vanished into thin air altogether, leaving behind only a serpentine beam of magic.

"Never have I seen such heroics, young one!" Rumios applauded, turning to face Jovan, "Truly, you *are* the true born Knight of Salvation."

As Armin crouched to collect the three arrows secured in the ground, his jaw dropped in astonishment at the credit being lavished upon Bourg. Had *the archer* not been the first to wake up, discover the attack, and thwart the attempt on the shepherd's life?

Jovan was pondering much the same as the archer and blushed beneath his helmet at the misunderstanding.

"It was the efforts of many." Jovan observed, "Mount up, Fellowship. Let us return the good shepherd to his homeport of Callistra."

"They shall have a lavish feast awaiting the arrival of the Knight of Salvation!" Rumios vowed, mounting Danavas alongside Jovan whilst the other heroes each mounted their steeds.

"Hey, Quick Draw," Helimslynch snorted as the others left. "I notice you weren't so quick on the string when your enchantress lady-friend was in danger! Great hunter indeed!"

"I could not kill a living thing." Armin announced, "Knowing Talian has inspired me against slaying even a murderous cobra."

"Knowing Talian has made you a wimp!" Helimslynch scoffed, dropping the now weathered copy of the Sacred Text into Swift's saddle sack. "Surrender your bow, arrows, and swords quietly, mighty archer; I won't tell a soul!"

Armin's eyes gazed at the retreating winged form of Talian once more. They then settled on the form of Rumios, still babbling in Jovan's ear about how he could have very well been acting alone. Inside, Armin's blood boiled over.

"We are falling behind, Brother Dwarf." Armin announced, ushering Swift forward.

From his seat atop Danavas, Rumios was continuously offering up praises to the Knight of Salvation and promising him many festivals and adulations once Trina was freed. Still, Jovan Bourg simply wasn't buying it. For all of the adulations and blessings being offered to the Knight of Salvation, he directed them to be shared with the Fellowship. Rumios was left powerless to tempt the Knight to take more praise than he deserved. If anything else, he was determined to accept *less* than he truly deserved. In the Knight's absence,

Rumios had detected the rising weakness in Armin; but that was *envy* where his specialty was *greed*. However, somewhere in the back of Rumios's mind, the command decision was made that he wasn't about to let Mynos simply continue where he had left off to manipulate envy. To weaken one member of the Fellowship was to weaken the Trinity. Weakening the Trinity would weaken the Knight. If anyone was going to receive the credit for the downfall of the Trinity *and* the Knight of Salvation, it would be Rumios!

Rumios coyly placed a hand to the tip of his staff and twin tendrils of darkness exploded into the air seeking to ensnare Armin in secret and plague his consciousness and heart in darkness and greed.

The serpentine strands of dark energy were inches away from striking Armin when Talian unleashed a cry from above.

"My magic detects a source of much darkness nearby!" the Guardian declared.

"Gorrenwrath?" Bourg asked, "Then we must make more haste than ever in reseating the noble shepherd. Kind sir..."

Rumios's concentration on his magic had been broken in all of the commotion. The strands of dark energy that had been sent to control Armin dissolved away to nothingness and Rumios's active staff unleashed a spell of its own outside of his control. Within moments, the illusory disguise of a shepherd's cane gave way to a staff twisted in darkness and a serpentine beam struck Rumios with such force as to knock him clean out of the saddle.

"Eh; the shepherd has fallen!" Helimslynch bellowed as Bob drew near the fallen Rumios, "What sort of magic is--?"

Even the Dwarven blacksmith swallowed the rest of the question as he beheld what happened next. The injured shepherd writhed freely on the ground before shedding his human skin and clothing as it dissolved away to scales. His human tongue gave way to a forked tongue. His dark locks of hair fell away. All that remained of the shepherd's human state was a magic staff twisted in darkness. The shepherd had given way to a powerless cobra in the middle of Scilia. Talian, having flown in low enough to see what had happened, reacted in shock before loosing a mystic tether from her side. Armin withdrew his bow once more. Helimslynch raised WarCleaver as the steeds circled their serpentine enemy.

"Hold." Jovan's baritone timbre instructed of his fellow riders; then, dismounting Danavas once more where he stomped the ground with a titanium boot that launched the cobra airborne once more, "What is your true name and your true purpose here? Who commands you?"

"Gorrenwrath commandsss..." the furthest approximation from a human voice hissed before giving way to no further human speech or actions at all. The cobra slithered and writhed for a few moments more, then unnaturally burst into flames of nothingness.

"The very wretched beast that Gorrenwrath has sent to mark our end," Bourg observed, "he has destroyed in its own failure."

"So, Brother Dwarf," Armin retorted, "it would appear that Gorrenwrath is no mere fairytale after all."

"Bah; Gorrenwrath may be real enough but I saw no mention of him in your Sacred Text either!" Helimslynch snapped.

"The threat is real; and whoever this man was, he was a disciple of Evil." Talian observed.

"She speaks the truth, friends." Bourg concluded, "Life for this Fellowship will not be an easy task. This quest is mine to undertake; the involvement of the Fellowship is up to each of you."

"The Dwarven general rides with you!" Helimslynch bellowed, beating WarCleaver against the ground.

"As do I." Talian added, "You will not face your trials alone."

"Then there are four of us." Armin concluded, "This Fellowship has taught me much of family."

Somewhere in the back of Bourg's mind, he knew that there was more than a sense of comradery that the Fellowship offered him but that was beside the point.

"Then we are as one." Bourg announced, "Let us press forward on this noble quest."

GLUTTONY

The sounds of much revelry and celebration rang from the halls like the church bells announcing Sunday services. The highly religious and noble leaders had gathered in honor of a day that marked the Son of the Cloth's fifth birthday and the day that his mother would be sworn in as the church's highest elder. She was blessed with such a distinction by holy lineage, as was reported in the Sacred Text. The fact that such a day coincided with her son's birthday was an afterthought. Her husband's absence at a day to honor her was an annoyance. Today marked a day to honor the political rising of Martilla Bourg and the tradition of the Sacred Text's teachings.

Food and drink flooded over all of the noble peoples of Trina in equal proportions as Martilla Bourg lapped up the adulations cast before her. She had, after all, earned them all. Her accomplishments, and her just reward, were as recorded in the Sacred Text. Some things were simply beyond the understanding of Maxim Bourg's unlearned mind and Martilla's special day was better off without him.

As adulations, food, drink, and good humor flowed freely off of the church walls, Jovan Bourg sat in a tiny corner of the room and gawked in confusion. These men and women were the church elders and noble political leaders. He had never seen them behave as they did that day. Was such odd behavior truly expected of the church leaders and politicians to fulfill the edicts of a Sacred Text that he was still too young to understand for himself?

Amidst the boy's ponderings, the door into the banquet hall burst open. Church leaders, nobles, and politicians leapt in start at the sudden noise. Had the uncleansed come to disrupt the church's celebration? Had one of their worshippers just interfered at an inopportune moment? Either way, the sounds of the joyous revelry silenced themselves as but a single man entered the room. He was not the unlearned searching to prove a point in protest, nor was he an unwise believer who had arrived at an ill time; he was both. Maxim Bourg had graced a celebration for his wife's achievements with his presence.

"You are using the fifth birthday of the Son of the Cloth to defile the church *grounds with such behavior as this?" Bourg demanded, taking his confused son to his own side.*

Here, Daz, the Archbishop of the temple of Lyr, rose from his seat.

"You would barge in here and accuse us of defiling our good and most Holy church?" Daz demanded.

"Restore your noble seat, Archbishop." Bourg interjected, taking his son, "I do apologize for interfering on this party, lords and ladies; but I do see before me plenty of leftovers to be divided up amongst the needy. Good day to all of you."

There, in the midst of the day to celebrate Martilla Bourg's political rise to power, Maxim Bourg stole off with his son and the remaining food and drink to be shared among the impoverished.

The mountain community of Lyr had once been one of such beauty that it housed only the noblest of politicians and religious leaders atop its peak. At the persistence of the Great War, however, even Lyr had given way to dust.

It had been five years prior that the community of unbelievers, seeking to add their unwise voices to noble council, had stormed the mountain of Lyr to deliver their disagreeable petition. In the wake of their arrival and reasonable dissention from the high and righteous politicians and leaders, most leaders had perished by nightfall. The once gorgeous, enviable grounds of Lyr lay to ruin beneath the bones of the departed noble politicians and the unsettled dust of death. Now the dust settled ravenously over the bones that had once marked a beautiful path to the Temple of Light. The Temple of Light, itself a place of former great authority, was cast into ruins of generations of violent, undeterred upheaval. The one room untouched by destruction remained the banquet hall; and in this hall resided the one remaining member of a self-righteous political class. Now, here he rested, a disheveled man of lost fortune as Martilla Bourg had taken his most highest position of religious distinction three decades past. The archbishop was left to dwell in devastation of lost power. The former archbishop dwelt in the vaulted banquet hall, trying to avoid the heavily decorated table that had represented his most humiliating offense on his last day in power. Still, he felt so cold, so weak, so...old. The food offered him strength, and the food came from...

The dust of hundreds of dead politicos flowed into the room and seemed to build up to form a humanoid form.

"You!" Daz managed meekly.

"You must partake of this glorious banquet that I have lain before you; it gives you strength." The dust humanoid announced, his voice a mixture of all of the dead politicians.

"No; I cannot." Daz trembled.

"If you want your strength and your youth back, you can." The humanoid rumbled..

Daz took a bite of food and sip of delicious wine; and his vigor was rejuvenated.

"I am strong once more!" Daz bellowed, "You have given me life!"

"And, as per our agreement, Archbishop," the humanoid concluded, "you deliver me the life of the Knight of Salvation."

"I am to destroy the Knight of Salvation for you?" Daz demanded, "Is Gorrenwrath not up to the challenge?"

With a swirling of dust, the glorious spread marking the table emptied itself. Then, within moments, an explosion of dust knocked the fallen archbishop's feeble form up against the nearest wall.

"To perform such a task is *beneath* the power of Gorrenwrath!" Gorrenwrath bellowed, "My disciples are charged to kill a pack of mortal warriors to pave the way for my continued destruction of Trina!"

"Restore my food and drink; renew my strength!" Daz pleaded, feebly.

With a dark, rumbling chuckle, the dust storm settled once more and the food and drink representing Daz's most humbling error reappeared, beckoning to him silently.

"Take up the food and drink that is yours to renew your strength and steer the Knight of Salvation to the path of his own destruction." Gorrenwrath instructed, "Cost your *successor* the life of her son."

Daz's successor, the Mother Superior. Misinterpretations of the Sacred

Text had cost Archbishop Daz what would have been rightly his until the day of his grave. That prestige and power had rested with the wrong person for three decades. Now, Daz's eyes burned with renewed hatred as he raised the crystal chalice to his lips.

"Jovan Bourg will pave the path to his own demise." Daz vowed. "The church's beloved Mother Superior will reveal herself at her true weakest in mourning her son's death. The people will recognize the utter shame that their Knight brought such destruction upon himself."

"What is rightfully yours shall be restored." Gorrenwrath declared. Such a grand promise rang with the empty speeches of each dead politician and noble lord of Lyr. Still, these were politicians and nobles who had supported Daz as the archbishop. Their words held merit once more. Daz's eyes burned with the renewed vigor of rejuvenated strength and as swiftly as Gorrenwrath had arrived in the form of dust, he departed in the same way.

The expedition paused in order to rest. Still, that was just fine with Armin Kinston. He had much reflection to do that he could not perform while the expedition was moving. Kinston knelt alongside a small stream that emptied into the nearby Callistra Sea. His quiver, bow, and blades lay abandoned nearby as he stared into the stream at his own reflection. Helimslynch could see that his "brother" was in a perplexed state and chose wisely to leave him be. Bourg, the Knight of Salvation, was plagued with contemplating their next move nearby. Talian, however, seemed to sense that she was needed whether Armin cared to admit it or not. She spread her magnificent wings and approached the Elf from behind. Only as she drew nearer did she realize that he was not staring into the stream. She was intruding on his time reading the Sacred Text. Still, by the time that Talian had realized her error in judgment, it was too late; the archer was disturbed.

"Forgive me, Elven archer." the Guardian announced herself as she landed at his side, "You seem troubled by something."

Armin only raised his eyes from the Sacred Text for but a moment, refusing to acknowledge that his current audience was a mere few steps away from him. Instead, he murmured his musings more to himself than to address the Guardian of his peoples.

That which is of this life
The passions of the heart and pride of personal wealth
Comes not from above but from Trina.[3]

"I fear that I do not understand." Talian confessed, "Should I leave you to your thoughts?"

"Fairest Talian," Armin addressed her, finally turning to face the visitor, "I-I have no business on this quest. My Dwarven brother has correctly observed of the Elven practice to worship our natural beauty and natural abilities as gifts from the Great Almighty without truly paying homage where it is due. The creature called Rumios sought to incite my foolish envy of noble Jovan Bourg. He nearly succeeded in steering me toward the greed of wanting to lap credit upon saving the beast's life for myself. I-I dare not reveal my greatest shame, even to you."

"Then I shall not ask you to again." Talian reassured him, "Your bow and your loyalty are as needed on these quests as Helimslynch's bravery and my nobility. However, the true success of this quest remains with the White Knight."

The decision rang from Jovan Bourg's slight baritone timbre that time was of the essence; the next object of their quest being Mount Lyr. In many ways, the elf welcomed the chance to prove his loyalty to the cause, if not the interruption.

"I thank you, fair Talian." Armin announced, scrambling back to his feet and tucking the Sacred Text away into his quiver, "You have indeed helped more than I could hope to confess. But, if I am to be of aid in the quest, there is much that I must work through for myself in the coming days. Noble Swift!"

Within moments, the mare advanced on his master and Armin flipped athletically into the steed's saddle. Beneath her ceremonial mask to conceal her beauty, Talian's face registered pity at the archer's expense. Still, she could not let that slow her. Elion, the horned falcon and her waif, swooped in from above once more and discovered his mistress's shoulder.

"It is not enough to observe the Knight of Salvation in his quest, my feathered friend." Talian observed, "Too we must keep the entirety of this expedition on the proper path as guides of wisdom."

"I am sure that the long-eared one would welcome any 'guidance' of yours woman!" Helimslynch's gravelly bark sounded from nearby.

Talian, midway into the air, lost her concentration and Elion took to the air in defense of his mistress at the sound of the new voice.

"You startled me, General of Dwarves." Talian rebuked her ally. "Please; what is this that you speak of so cavalierly?"

"You'll see, winged one." Helimslynch grunted, "Forward, Bob!"

The members of the Fellowship fell into line once more and pressed on their noble journey passed the village of Callistra toward the devastated mountain peaks of Lyr. The Guardian remained hopelessly confused as she spread her majestic wings once more and fluttered to catch up to the rest of the troupe. She only hoped that, in time, the answer to her latest question would dawn on her. Armin hope that, when that time came, he would have grown passed his less than professional feelings about her.

From his place of imprisonment in the hallowed halls of the once majestic palace, Daz gazed through the rising dust that had announced the death of all of his political allies. As the dust shifted as if disturbed by a silent breeze, it revealed the Fellowship's quest toward Mount Lyr. Talian's magic had served the Knight and the Trinity well in detecting the presence of ancient evil. After his near defeat years before and the fact that the enchantress had sensed his presence in his agent, Rumios, Gorrenwrath had counted on Talian detecting him in Lyr. Furthermore, if his agent Daz wanted to know the thirst of eternal youth and taste of the outside world ever again, the fallen archbishop would know what to do.

Within moments, the ravenous dust that had been the result of such violence and destruction settled to form a nearby table, complete with food and drink. Daz eyed the table hungrily and ignored his own spread to approach the wine goblet on the neighboring table. Still, before he could take a drink, the liquid contents seemed to vanish, only to replenish when he put the goblet back. Still, in the liquid's absence, a glistening golden band did remain. As Daz scooped up the tiny band questioningly, he recognized it immediately and his face registered confusion.

"The fabled Ring of Renecar?" Daz demanded questioningly, "If this is truly the ring of lore, it will only serve to increase the destructive potential of the winged one's powers!"

"Renecar's deadly ring is very real and it is truly before you." Gorrenwrath hissed, "The destructive potential of the Guardian's powers will be increased one thousand fold, as will her temptation to utilize their awesome potential. However, such increased power does wager a high price. Her increased power draws directly from the spirit vision that allows her to trace my movements."

"Whether she can detect you or not, you will meet again." Daz insisted, "Is it wise to gift her with such destructive potential?"

"For a Guardian, that is the highest price of all, foolish one." Gorrenwrath reassured him, "The Celestial Guardians are direct messengers from Heaven. They gather their powers from that which is light, *not* the darkness that is destruction."

Daz nodded in silent understanding at what appeared to be a room devoid of any other being. All that he needed do was wait out the Fellowship; they would partake of excess food and drink of their own accords, and he would be free of his deadening prison.

The steeds were left at the base of the mountain to graze and faithfully wait out their masters. Their riders determinedly scaled Mount Lyr, once fabled as a place of beauty set aside for only the highly religious and revered politicians. Now, the dust and bones of deceased church leaders and politicos blanketed the ground in a nearly impassable terrain to the one last remaining building. The temple housing the fallen Archbishop Daz still stood. Upon reaching the top of Lyr's summit and his destination, Jovan Bourg removed his helmet and collapsed to one knee right in front of what remained of his party.

"The dust and bones beneath our feet once represented our highest and most revered leaders." Bourg reflected, "I have distinct memories of each of them being there to celebrate my mother's rise to highest church elder. Now, they are dust, bones, and remnants to be trampled upon in our path to the last standing temple of Lyr."

"Seems appropriate enough to me that the people should be trampling upon their politicians now!" Helimslynch barked, stamping his foot intentionally against the ground.

"Is it so appropriate for them to have died by violence from your fellow unbelievers?" Armin demanded.

Helimslynch's beard bristled, his muscles tensed, and his eyes radiated untapped fire at the charge.

"Violence came to our politicians' stomping grounds because they refused to listen to the whims of the commoners anymore. Their cozy nook atop Mount Lyr begot such indifference to the troubles of the commoner!" Helimslynch bristled. "You can see for yourself, Brother among Elves, what has become of their happy homestead! And, no, the violence and horrors of war are never an appropriate first resort. A misfortune that the believer and unbeliever shares in common with one another is the loss of vision of what the price-tag of an ages-old war truly is."

"Then you are a weaponsmith and Dwarven savage who hates war?" Armin asked, his eyes coated in silent laughter.

Here, Helimslynch turned to face his audience.

"I am a *black*smith who was only ever appreciated for my weapons and a Dwarf who is not so savage as prejudice would lead you to believe." He grunted.

In the midst of the exchange, Talian extended a hand for silence between the two allies. Within moments, Elion swooped in once more and perched on her shoulder with a screech. Talian nodded in understanding and stroked her winged ally on the head affectionately.

"Thank you, faithful Elion." Talian declared; then, to Bourg: "The undamaged temple rests just ahead. It remains occupied by one former archbishop."

"Daz." Bourg murmured the name with a nod of understanding before replacing his helmet, "Onward, Fellowship. The temple remains untouched by this destruction and is but mere steps away."

As the Knight of Salvation led the divine Trinity in the direction of the unblemished building, Talian shuddered where she stood. Her powers had detected some unchecked Evil nearby. Still, Elion had already announced that their destination was ahead and the only other person on Lyr Mountain was Daz. Besides, the others were already several steps ahead and there was still the distinct possibility that the fact that Talian was standing on top of the deceased bones of those who were killed by war had triggered a false vision. Nonetheless, Talian didn't have to leave any potential evil unchecked before she continued. Within moments, a mystic barrier of energy surrounded the mountaintop, impassable by any outside force. With the protective barrier in place, Talian spread her mystic wings and flew to join her allies. From his place of imprisonment inside the banquet hall, Daz saw the Fellowship's approach through the shifting dust. The heroes were approaching, the table was appropriately decorated for their arrival, and the hour of Archbishop Daz's freedom was close at hand...

Even the steps leading up to the door of the unblemished building were untouched by unsettled bones and dust. If the rest of Mount Lyr had given way to ruin, the Temple of Light remained a beautiful manifestation of the former glory that it had once represented. Armin and Bourg paused momentarily to admire the building, deliberating whether or not it should be tainted with their presence. Still, with a mighty swing from WarCleaver, Helimslynch battered open the doors to reveal the hallway.

"The fallen archbishop isn't going anywhere himself!" Helimsylnch reasoned to the unasked question as he shouldered his axe determinedly. There was a moment when it seemed as though Armin was ready to upbraid the Dwarf for his insolence. Still, the Knight of Salvation opened his mouth first.

"Discard your weapons at the door." Bourg instructed, laying the Icarus aside, "This is a house of worship."

Helimslynch started to spit out a guffaw of protest before reasoning with himself that the Knight of Salvation had placed aside his blade, then the archer with his weapons. These were clearly believers who were willing to lead by their own examples. When Talian placed aside her mystic tether and staff, Helimslynch cast aside WarCleaver and entered behind the line.

Entering the Great Hall, the Fellowship was greeted on all sides by the beauty of the glory that the church had once represented. Upon facing down the former greatness, even Helimslynch appeared slightly impressed by the grandeur. The greatness of the once holy hall even drew Talian and Armin closer together.

"A beautiful sight, no?" Talian asked.

"A magnificent *promise*, fair Guardian." Armin amended, "Brother Dwarf, what you see before you is what the church...*should* promise."

"Take ease, everyone." Bourg interjected, "Great, unblemished beauty does surround us; while the rest of Mount Lyr is in ruin. My question is why? I see no danger for your summons to have led us here, Talian. I also do not see the archbishop who asked us."

"You are admiring the wrong area of this precious House of Worship, Son of the Church." An aged, pleasant voice announced as an elderly man approached from an open chamber, "Today, a former Head of Church is graced by the presence of the Knight of Salvation. You have grown since we last crossed paths, Son of the Cloth."

"And, to hear the tale of this first meeting, you've sobered up since then too!" Helimslynch barked haughtily, prompting a jab in the ribs from Armin.

"Ah, yes; the Trinity." Daz declared, stepping passed the Knight of Salvation, "It is an honor to be graced with your presence in my home. I had my doubts, as the Sacred Text never identified who should represent this Trinity, nor the time of its arrival. However, I trust in the Knight of Salvation's judgment."

"Good to know; because we're it, mister!" Helimslynch spat, crossing his arms before his chest.

"Forgive our loud friend and our intrusion on your hallowed grounds,

Archbishop." Armin announced, "Our ethereal Guardian sensed great danger here."

"The rage of Dwarven kind has preceded the great General's arrival, mighty hunter." Daz chuckled, "As to the sense of threat that has drawn you here, I am afraid that it was merely spiritual unrest in the souls of all of those who have passed before me. So as not to waste your trip or your time in this quest, however, you are welcome to join me at table with the benefit of your company. Come; this way into the Great Dining Hall. I promise that I will provide each of you with your fill for the tiring journey ahead of you."

"Heh; today this quest delivers me to a believer-type who's willing to give credit and due respect to the great General and to fill his stomach in one sitting!" Helimslynch barked, "Hustle up, 'mighty hunter'."

"Indeed, it would be a high promise that offers you *your* fill of food." Armin chuckled, falling in step behind him, "Spare us some scraps, Brother Dwarf!"

As the Dwarf and Elf disappeared into the Great Banquet Hall behind the former Archbishop, the White Knight of Salvation and Talian hung back for a moment.

"You are distressed, winged one?" Bourg asked.

"Yes; despite the destruction surrounding Mount Lyr, this Temple was never touched." Talian murmured, "Alas, I know that my powers detected a threat."

"Mount Lyr is consumed in the blood, bones, and dust of restless, unfulfilled politicians and fallen religious leaders." Bourg observed, disappearing in the direction of the open room, "Our host awaits our arrival in the Banquet Hall."

For the briefest moment, Talian was left alone in the outer hall, save for Elion's presence. For the briefest moment, the horned falcon remained perched on his mistress's shoulder as the others disappeared into the vaulted inner chamber. The blacksmith and general had had his record in combat stroked and the archer had been heralded as a great hunter. Therefore, two members of the Trinity sworn to protect the Knight of Salvation had led him into the dining hall.

"I do not like this, friend Elion." Talian admitted, the magic in her hands continuing to flash forewarnings as she entered the hall.

The beauty and glory of the temple's entryway was clearly only over-shadowed by the beauty and glory radiating from the Banquet Hall. All of the church's former glory reflected and radiated off of the walls like a beckon call that all who entered would find rest. Furthermore, as if the majesty of an undressed Banquet Hall did not hold enough appeal, this Hall had two lavishly decorated tables. It was enough food for an army and certainly enough for the Fellowship to take their fill. Whilst Armin and Helimslynch were still stunned speechless, Jovan found his voice first.

"Archbishop Daz, we are more than thankful for your hospitality; but we cannot possibly accept such a lavish feast." Bourg announced, "It is so much; nearly as much as when you--."

"You refuse my hospitality, youngling?" Daz interjected, his eyes radiating offense, "Then you are no friend of the Cloth; much less its *Son*. You and your Fellowship have no business here."

"On behalf of the Dwarves of Iron Mountain, I have plenty of business here; *I* will feast!" Helimslynch barked.

"That the church might continue to protect the Elven people of Dawn Valley, I shall dine with you as well." Armin announced.

"You can no longer threaten the loss of the church's protection, Archbishop." Bourg declared, "But as a token of the church's good grace and respect, I will proudly dine with a former leader of the Cloth."

"Your presences would be most appreciated!" Daz announced, raising his glass in a toast devoid of his earlier rage, "And you, winged Guardian of all of Trina? You can consider it an opportunity to protect the Trinity and I will even offer you a beautiful gift."

The more that Daz spoke in such humbling tones, building the egos of his visitors, the more that the mystic energies of forewarning burned within Talian. As Daz passed a preselected chalice to her, the mystic Guardian's foresight reached fruition. Something had to be done about this; even at the risk of offending a former church elder.

"My humblest apologies, Archbishop Daz; while we do certainly appreciate your generous hospitality presented before us, I fear that I simply cannot accept…" Talian protested just before her eyes fell upon the glistening golden band in the bottom of the empty chalice, "The…fabled… RING…OF…RENECAR?"

"Surely you have heard of its great power to enhance your magic by one thousand fold?" Daz announced, holding the chalice out to her encouragingly. "For you, beautiful Guardian. The ring represents great power, certainly enough to drive Gorrenwrath's evil from this world. That is why the Fellowship was assembled, yes?"

Within moments, the mystic ring loosed itself from the bottom of the chalice and affixed itself on the Guardian's hand as if that had been where it had always belonged. As the ring affixed itself to her finger, Talian could feel her powers increasing. Furthermore, as her powers increased, the forewarning flash dissipated. For the briefest moment, Talian was no longer concerned with the loss of her spirit vision. Her power was instantly great due to the new gift; certainly great enough to rid Trina of Gorrenwrath.

"Let us eat and drink to the certain defeat of the ancient Evil that plagues this world!" Daz declared, draining his chalice before focusing on the succulent feast placed before him.

Before long, the Fellowship followed suit and sat and dined and drank over one another's company. All of the while, Gorrenwrath silently observed through his agent's eyes as the heroic Fellowship gave way to the temptation of gluttony. Even as the rest of the Fellowship ate their fill and more, however, Bourg would only eat in small portions. Talian had sensed that something was wrong long before and Bourg was starting to sense it for himself.

"Fellowship," he announced, pushing his chair back from its place at the table, "I believe that each of us has had our fill at this sitting. We appreciate your hospitality, Daz. The church will know of your generosity. However, we must be leaving if only to continue on our quest."

As the Knight of Salvation pushed back his chair and rose, only Talian would follow suit, her hands brimming with increased magical energy.

Armin and Helimslynch, however, continued to dine, oblivious to the fact that anyone had risen from the table. Daz, however, was not oblivious to their actions as he leapt up from his seat with far more energy than his old bones should have given out.

"You cannot leave!" Daz bellowed, the airs of his former glory replaced once more by rage, "I-I have not been told of your adventures so far, young ones. Entertain an old gentleman with tales of your quest so far."

The words were a reasonable request. However, the tone was too pleading to be natural. The heroes' stay was no longer a request of a former church leader but the demand of an embittered old man. Bourg turned and faced down the elderly former minister as he exhibited strength, energy, and rage that would rival that of men half his age. Talian had warned the Knight of Salvation that she had sensed trouble before and he had not filed her warning under proper consideration. Now the heroes sat in the dining hall, surrounded by food and drink. It was exactly the same temptation that had caused the ministers' and politicians' most public and humiliating fall from grace as they had partaken of too much food and drink under the scrutiny of the five-year-old Son of the Cloth mere hours before his mother was officially pronounced Mother Superior of Trina.

"Daz," Bourg murmured, approaching the minister for as much confidentiality as possible, "you are not well."

As Daz sputtered and mused, the dust of unsettled spirits swirled around him.

"You!" Daz exclaimed, "You will partake of your fill!"

"I have Archbishop; you have been more than generous to us." Jovan announced, "What has happened to you, kindly Archbishop?"

Daz's eyes flashed in rage.

"I will not be free of this imprisoning Banquet Hall until I have seen the Good Knight of Salvation purge more than his fill of meal!" Daz shouted. Even amidst the chorus of shouts, Armin and Helismlynch did not recover from their posthypnotic stupor. Only a blast of mystic energy that destroyed their table and ground all of the beautiful place settings there upon to ashes restored their senses.

In the absence of food, Helimslynch and Armin snapped back to attention and rose up alongside their allies, longing for their weapons again. They had each been deceived by the stroking of their individual egos and the feast lain before their eyes and stomachs. They would not allow the evidence of their near fall from grace to remain unturned.

"My table; my food and drink!" Daz sobbed.

"No, Archbishop; that was *our* table and its trimmings." Talian amended, casting a sweeping gesture right in front of her, "*That* is your table."

Within moments, another beam of energy emanated into the air and cast Daz's table and its fixings into the same ruins as the Fellowship's. A cold wind echoed through the dining hall and Archbishop Daz no longer appeared so much younger and stronger than his years. He appeared so many centuries older than his recorded age and just as feeble.

"At a young age, I had the misfortune of paying witness to a once great leader's fall from grace." Bourg reflected, sadly, "That man who the church once respected with its highest regards meant to allure me into the same trap where he could witness my collapse. To free yourself from your own prison, you meant to see the destruction of the White Knight of Trina's Salvation. Fellowship, we leave this beauteous prison that we might return to our steeds and our journey."

"Fetch my mighty WarCleaver and this rotten house won't have to keep standing much longer!" Helimslynch spat, leading the way out of the Banquet Hall.

"No; there's no need to return here and deliver more violence to Mount Lyr." Armin insisted, "We will let the once great Archbishop live out his last few years knowing that he meant to destroy the Fellowship, had failed, and must continue to live with his own self-destructive failures."

"He may continue to live with his failures," Talian concluded, her voice suddenly contorted in rage, "but that doesn't mean that he needs to see freedom ever again!"

As the heroes reached the mountain outside of the temple once more and collected their weapons, Talian performed one last feat of magic before her astonished audience. Utilizing only the magic of an ethereal

Guardian, Talian sealed the church doors magically. Elion, sensing what his mistress was doing, screeched in consternation while Armin gawked in silent wonder. Still, neither might as well have been there until Talian declared that her work was done and Daz would be forever sealed in the temple. Without a word, Talian spread her majestic wings and took to the air to lead the way back down the mountain. Thus left the heroes wondering in astonishment what had driven a divine Guardian of Trina into sealing any man, evil or not, in an early tomb.

Daz saw the closing doors and sensed the mystic seals falling into place. Still, the conniving Archbishop had been robbed of his youth and would not be denied his liberty. The elderly former minister rushed feebly toward the doors. The ruined Banquet Hall that had been his prison to remind him of his crushing temptation and the main doors were his escape to freedom. Still, Daz hadn't even fled the Banquet Hall when a giant wall of dust with the consistency of concrete solidified in his face, forcing him to slam into the barrier. As the minister stumbled back a couple of steps, his feet were caught in the dust of his former politicos and he was sinking fast into what was undoubtedly quicksand. Within moments, the red dust that now blanketed Mount Lyr as a grim reminder of a time long forgotten surged forward and sought to suffocate the failed Archbishop.

"Lord Gorrenwrath, show mercy on an elderly agent of your conquest!" Daz pleaded.

"Mercy; for failure?" the sinister voice demanded, amplified by the sounds of each voice of Mount Lyr's deceased members. "You must have me confused for some weaker deity!"

"No, my liege; n-never!" Daz whimpered. "I will serve only you!"

"Then it was in my name that you committed the cardinal sin of failure!" Gorrenwrath mused, "Do not fear a repeat offense following your repentance. The cost of the first offense yields the highest price."

"Lord Gorrenwrath, I beseech your kindness!" Daz begged. "I very nearly lured each member of the great Trinity to failure!"

"You were supposed to humble the *Knight*; not his worthless Trinity!" Gorrenwrath seethed, "They are three but they are weak. To destroy them accomplishes nothing so long as the Knight of Salvation presses on his road!"

"Lord Gorrenwrath..." Daz whimpered, his age revealing his frailty.

"You are quibbling before me!" Gorrenwrath raged as the great cloud of the dust of dead swirled around Daz and encased him, strangling his pleas.

As the dust settled, only a skeleton remained of the late, fallen archbishop. In his life, he had been a captive of sin. Now he was a captive of death at the hands of an invisible Evil. The Fellowship pressed on on another journey. To Gorrenwrath, that was unacceptable...

SLOTH

The exhaustive heat of a Harvest Summer settled upon Trina's great shores. However, the greatest friends of the Church and its most valiant soldiers were hard at work in the fields. From inside of the Holy place, Jovan Bourg, now seven, snuck a glance up from his studies of the Sacred Text. Out the nearest window, he watched the workers in curiosity as they toiled the fields surrounding the church. Surely, they had much respect for their Mother Superior's ministry or else they would find better things to do on a warm summer's day. The warmer the sun got, the more workers arrived to toil the fields. This certainly perplexed young Jovan Bourg more than anything written in the Sacred Text and he scanned the room for a direct answer as to what had driven such work. Mother Superior would have known the answer but she was no where to be found. Joto, the church's servant since Bourg's crib time, however, stood ever at the ready. He was employed not outside of the church as the others but in the corner of the room as a causal observer of the boy's studies.

"Loyal Joto," Jovan piped up, "why do the soldiers and our parishioners toil as they do?"

"They are friends of the Church, noble Son of the Cloth." Joto announced, surprised that the question should even cross the boy's mind. "Return to your studies."

"The parishioners work while the Son of the Church does nothing for betterment." Bourg observed, going to close the Sacred Text that he might go outdoors and help. Still, he was stopped by a hand on his shoulder.

"It is the Day of the Sabbath." Joto announced, "Today, you rest, save for your studies."

"It is not the Sabbath Day for them?" Jovan asked, by now hopelessly confused.

Joto afforded a slight chuckle to hide the grimace threatening to go above his face mask.

"You are very curious, boy!" Joto applauded. "I shall explain more of the rules of the Sabbath once your studies are complete. For now, simply take me at my word that it is the day of the Sabbath."

"It is an excuse to be lazy and drive servants!" a male voice thundered from out in the hall outside of the child's room. Within moments, Maxim Bourg forced open the bedroom and entered to join his son before Joto could prevent the soldier of the unbelievers from entering.

"Maxim," Joto hissed, "do not fill the boy's head with your grievances. You are a soldier of unbelief!"

"Today, let my role be as my boy's father, friend Joto." Maxim pleaded, "I will take him out into the fields that he may see what life is like out there. It is what he has asked you. I will not allow my son to be as blind as his mother; nor to work so hard as to only know your life, friend Joto."

Joto went to protest once more; then nodded in silent agreement of the father's plea...

The mountain of Nardot was constantly covered in frost, cast to a part of Trina where the sun never shown. None traveled to Nardot willingly; the Dwarves who had once called it their home had become the colonists of Iron Mountain many centuries before. Those who were sent to live in Nardot as a special purgatory for the vilest of unbelievers did not live for long. Each punished member was plagued by the white death of pneumonia or cast into an icy tomb where they stood. Such was the punishment reserved for those who did the most offense to the Holy Place. Only one humanoid soul continued to move as silently and stealthily as the cold that entombed his body to conceal his movements from sight. Silax appeared to be as frozen as anyone else; yet he lived, save for his years of slumber. Today marked one of those days when the bitter frost would raise him from his desired rest once more.

The haze of snow, ice, frost, and cold hung lazily on the air as a grim reminder of the permanent rest that had befallen all who traversed Nardot. As the frost settled over the mountaintops, a large Polaron raised its head lazily from his paws before the frigid haze of sloth got the better of him once more. A nearby family of Sels woke just enough to huddle closer together, then they too went back to sleep, grumbling lazily in their high-pitched barks. In a nearby cave, the only humanoid form that truly had life on the mountain anymore peered out over the animals of Nardot. In his rest, Silax's body blended in with the cavern walls. Only one sinister force ever had the authority to disturb Silax from his frigid hibernation.

"The Fellowship approaches." Silax mused, apparently to himself. "My master fears them and beckons me that they fall to temptation. Bah; a pack of mortal dogs preparing a threat to the 'great and mighty' Gorrenwrath! However, the peace of my eternal rest will only be restored once those fools join me in it!"

With a lazy sweep of his hand, Silax urged the mist of frost to intensify experimentally. The polar creatures who shared his mountain did not rise again but returned to their lazy hibernations beneath the renewed Arctic haze. Surely, the same results would befall a few humans who knew nothing of the cold of Nardot. The mist would make short work of the Fellowship, 'Holy' or no. Silax was free to return to his rest while the mist did his bidding. The lord of Nardot glanced lazily around at the crystalline stalagmites surrounding him on the ground. It was only moments before his crystalline body became as one of its neighbors to allow its master to observe his surroundings in peace once again...

Neither Helimyslynch nor Armin had much to say to anyone as the Fellowship left Lyr and traversed along the fruitful plains of Anon. Anytime Armin did have anything to say, it was the Elvish practice of praising his gifts and his looks and confusing that for worshipping his Great Almighty. When Helimslynch spoke, it was to boast of his own abilities or to speak against the Believers. Their visit to Lyr, however, had not been one of the more promising examples of their petty human meagerness. The hunter and warrior had allowed their egos to be stroked. Now that their fellow travelers had paid witness to the very nearest that both men had ever come to falling to temptation, their egos were still significantly bruised.

Jovan caught the accidental vibes of his fellow travelers and wished that he might make any needed repairs to their spirits as the quest pressed on. Still, he could not. He could reaffirm their contributions to the Fellowship and reassure them that everyone fell at times. Still, the final repair to their spirits would be theirs to make. Besides, no one would admit it, but a pair of bruised egos amidst the group that had been assembled to keep the Knight of Salvation on a just path was the least of the groups' concerns. It had, after all, been the Celestial Guardian of ALL of Trina's peoples who had taken her enhanced powers and used them to try to seal a man away in a permanent prison. No matter what evil was in his heart, such drastic action seemed uncalled for. Still, no one was quite sure how to approach that concern.

Talian toyed with the Ring of Renecar on her finger. The very device that had enhanced her powers had oddly blinded her spirit vision. Still, a few minor adjustments could always restore her mystical sixth sense back to normal. With her spirit vision restored and her powers increased, the planet of Trina would indeed mark Gorrenwrath's final stand! Had that not been why the Fellowship had assembled in the first place?

"Talian." A concerned voice entered her thoughts, snapping her out of her dreams of the day of Gorrenwrath's destruction.

"Yes?" she demanded, the back of her mind working at double-speed to place the voice that had called her name, "W-What is it, Armin?"

The Elven archer had heard how the Celestial Guardian had originally spoken to him and was almost stunned beyond finishing his thought. Still, he had already started the thought; and Talian was just important enough to him for him to finish it.

"Are you alright?" Armin asked of Talian, "I-I worry about you after the past two confrontations with the evil ones."

"How do you mean, Elvish one?" Talian asked, the faintest tone of bitterness returning to her voice as if challenging Armin to complete his thought. Before he could live up to the challenge, Armin took a moment to reorganize his words and thoughts. However, the effort to rethink his approach was for naught. It wasn't two seconds later that his original thoughts, verbatim, were delivered loud, proud, punitive, and in the rough grumble of a Dwarven general.

"You tried to kill a man back at the temple!" Helimslynch crowed, triumphantly.

Talian's wings flapped with sufficient force that they might have beaten the feathers off as she arched her back momentarily before regaining her composure. As for Armin, he whipped around to face the knee-high general and blacksmith.

"You would have gladly not only attempted the same but finished the job if you had gotten ahold of your rotting axe!" the archer snapped.

"Aye; I did not say that I was not proud of the fair lady's attempt." Helimslynch sneered, "But, since you brought it up, let us test my 'rotting' axe against your precious arrows!"

"She has heard your say." Bourg announced, "My apologies, Talian, but the archer raises an intriguing curiosity."

Talian admired the golden band that had enhanced her powers for a moment longer.

"I-I cannot explain it." Talian declared, "The Ring of Renecar has gifted me so much intense power and...I could not keep it contained. Jovan, I blindly used my powers with the intent to harm a man!"

"A man who was clearly an agent of Gorrenwrath!" Helimslynch barked, "Furthermore, from where I was standing, you were aiming your hocus-pocus at the door instead of the demon!"

"Thank you for that, Helimslynch." Bourg interjected, "You addressed the ring as 'Renecar,' didn't you, Talian? The legends did whisper something about the ring's origins. I confess that I do not remember what..."

Within moments, a haze of ice and frost materialized in the middle of the Anon Plains, threatening the crops and blocking the Fellowship's path. Danavas reared up and loudly protested the sudden arrival of the freezing mist. Armin promptly draped a pair of blankets over him and Swift. Talian did all that she could to fly through the mist but eventually landed with Elion right beside her. Helimslynch spat where he sat astride Bob.

"A warm summer's breeze!" he scoffed.

"Perhaps if you were higher off of the ground, you would better feel the full brunt of this frigid mist?" Armin retorted, adjusting his bow and quiver of arrows to avoid them being damaged by the cold. "We should bed down for the night. The mist will surely be gone by dawn."

"I fear that the full brunt of this mist is still waiting for us atop Nardot, the Mountain of Frost. It very rarely burdens the rest of Trina without natural causes." Bourg observed, "I would consider the hand of Gorrenwrath or one of his disciples dictating this peculiarity. Talian, what says your ethereal spirit vision?"

"I—" Talian replied, straining with such ferocity that she finally exhausted her powers and collapsed against the oncoming mist of ice right into Armin's waiting arms, "—I really am not sure. My spirit vision has... left me somehow."

"It is too cold for Talian and the steeds to weather this journey any longer, Jovan." Armin declared, setting Talian gently astride Swift and wrapping her gingerly in a blanket. "We shall investigate these happenings in the morrow."

"By the morrow, the Anon Plains could be plagued with destruction from such cold." Bourg insisted, "The steeds have carried us far this day and Talian is clearly ailed. I will investigate the frosty purgatory of Nardot personally. Each of us has weathered a trying quest so far and those who wish to rest may do so with my blessings."

Bourg adjusted the Icarus in its hilt and checked the crystalline crucifix around his neck before pressing on his journey in the direction of Nardot. He was barely two steps away from the encampment before the Knight of Salvation could hear Helismlynch following him with short, determined strides. Several steps later, Armin rejoined the expedition as well. He was satisfied that Talian would heal and could go forward with the latest expedition with her blessings to guide him.

As the rays of dawn did all that they could to penetrate the haze of freezing sluggishness, the heroes had only recently begun their ascent of Nardot. As they attempted the climb, it was Helimslynch who seemed the most perturbed by the sudden chill hanging in the air around the heroes.

"Who are the inhabitants of this Nardot and why are they burdened with such a chilling frost?" the mountain Dwarf demanded, very nearly losing his footing a third time against the bitter cold. Before he could fall, however, Helimslynch caught a golden bow in one hand and was hoisted easily back to Nardot's ledge.

"Your footing is not so much to you away from the furnace of Iron Mountain, is it, Brother Dwarf?" Armin chuckled through his shivers. "Please, friend Jovan, regale us with the tale of the inhabitants of Nardot. Do they have natural fur to protect them from such a frost?"

"I wish that the matter was as light-hearted as you have been led to believe, my friend." Bourg observed, his soft-spoken baritone revealing a legitimate sense of pain in his forthcoming words. "Nardot is a frozen purgatory that the church has set aside for its most militant enemies of the cloth. Not even the Dwarves are cast here anymore. The lucky people restricted to Nardot die swiftly of the White Death. Those who are not so fortunate live just long enough to feel the pain of being entombed in ice."

"Enemies of the cloth, they have called them?" Helimslynch bellowed, "You mean..."

"Unbelievers, my little friend; societal outcasts that the church has exhausted its dealings with." Bourg explained, "Regrettably, the church has less energy for its dealings with unbelievers of late."

"And where in your book of fairytales does it advise leaving the disbeliever to a mountaintop to freeze?" Helimslynch demanded.

"Helimslynch..." Armin began to chide him.

"The *Sacred Text* makes no mention of where it is man's burden to judge men to court-decided purgatory." Bourg interjected, "However, its pages mention plenty about aiding society, forgiving those who have wronged you, and opening doors to acceptance."

"You are chiding me to *forgive* the offenses of those who would condemn their brothers to a White Death?" Helimslynch demanded, "I have accepted much of your murmurings from your old book throughout this voyage, Son of *Church Linen!*"

"The Son of the *Cloth* thanks you for your patience throughout this voyage. May you go down in history as a great warrior and noble ally." Bourg reflected, "I would hardly call it my place to advise the Dwarven community to do anything until the church should learn to practice forgiveness and open its doors to acceptance. Nardot's peak is but a short continuation away."

Within moments, the expedition reached the summit of Mount Nardot. As the frigid mist expanded into its mightiest, the heroes were beckoned to give way to lethargy and give up their quest. However, under the guidance of the White Knight of Salvation, the Fellowship would not abandon their latest expedition. Bourg thought that Gorrenwrath's hand was in the mist and was determined to find out for certain.

"Hold fast, friends." Jovan warned. "If this frigid mist does not persuade us to idleness while we wait for it to clear, it just may freeze us to death first."

"Then it may just have to try **freezing** us!" Helimslynch vowed, "Am I right, Brother of Pretty Elves?"

"These anomalies can certainly try to freeze the two of you," Armin quipped, "However, neither sloth nor the White Death will prevent me from returning to Talian!"

Such a pronouncement elicited a knowing chuckle from Helimslynch. From beneath his helmet, the Knight of Salvation adopted a look of concern. Between the threats of temptation toward greed, gluttony, and sloth, even Jovan Bourg had bought into enough of the church's teachings to sense the pattern forming. Furthermore, it was Armin who was straying dangerously close to the threat of *lust* without any provocation from an agent of evil.

A low growl from nearby interrupted Jovan's thoughts. It was a noise barely loud enough to overpower the roaring winds that delivered the haze of frozen sloth over Nardot. However, it was definitely a growl. No sooner had Jovan grasped blindly for the Icarus in case he needed to defend himself than that low growl became an ear shattering roar which prompted each member of the Fellowship to action.

"A Polaron!" Helimslynch barked, raising WarCleaver with pride. "Let us see how this foul beast likes the taste of my WarCleaver before it should ever experience the taste of my flesh!"

"Hold back, Brother Dwarf, and we will engage the creature from a distance!" Armin declared, already prepping his bow before the frosty haze could damage it.

"If you would both kindly hold your ground, we may not have to engage this Polaron at all." Jovan insisted, already raising the Icarus before the native creature could charge. Seeing the weapon, the Polaron arched its massive back and began to charge, the fur of its coat protecting it against the oncoming mist of sloth. Still, before the creature could strike, Bourg inserted the blade of the Icarus into the ice. Lo and behold, the Polaron paused and reached out with its paw. The massive creature was strong as a scavenger, but couldn't recognize the notion of leaving a straight line charge to go around the smallest barrier.

It wasn't a moment later that the readymade barrier between the Knight of Salvation and his predator revealed another purpose to the Fellowship's cause. The sun's rays that had been struggling to fight their way through the haze of laziness soon found the blade of the Icarus. As the Polaron tried to negotiate how to reach the Knight of Salvation, the light striking the blade intensified into a glowing cross. As the sunlight burned against the cross, it blinded the advancing Polaron to the point of driving it to either attack blindly or retreat. Even as the accompanying members of the Fellowship waited with drawn weapons, the Polaron chose to retreat even as the glistening cross not only drove the creature away but burned away some of the haze of the fog of laziness as well.

"Savage white-back!" Helimslynch grunted, his vigorous fighting spirit becoming restored in the dissipating mist, "Too bad it didn't stay to fight!"

"The mist has dulled the animals to laziness." Bourg explained, unearthing the Icarus from the ice and replacing it in its hilt. "Had we not been invading its home, it would have never approached us. It has gone to tell others like it to continue in their lazy slumber. Onward."

"What other animals lurk in these mountains, Knight of Salvation?" Armin asked.

"Did the mighty hunter forget to study his surroundings?" Helimslynch chortled. "Only Sels, loud, happy pups!"

"Indeed." Bourg confirmed, "The Polarons and Sels do not freeze to death beneath the mist of frost. They are merely weakened and more prone to laziness. Any people sent to Nardot to live were not so fortunate. We now must figure out why the Nardot mists are no longer restrained to the mountains."

"But the Icarus burned some of the mist away." Armin announced.

"A temporary remedy, friend Armin." Bourg observed. "If the mists of haziness once restricted only to Nardot have left the mountains, the haze can surely rebuild upon itself."

"You truly do believe of an evil hand guiding these anomalies, don't you?" Helimslynch demanded.

"Yes; it is unnatural for the Nardot Mist to move on its own. For it to descend upon the Anon Plains in such a relentless manner, it would require direction. I sense Gorrenwrath's hand in this as a desperate attempt to lure us to the failure of sloth." Bourg reflected, "Press forth, noble allies. The forbidding Frost Caverns of Nardot are just ahead. The mist cannot allure us to the mistake of laziness in there."

"Indeed, but we can still certainly **freeze**!" Armin insisted.

"Then, we just may be entombed in ice in the memory that we tried our very best to save Trina." Bourg observed. "Perhaps, on the day that someone succeeds against Gorrenwrath and his sinister agents, they will remember those who were martyred before them before they fall to deadly temptation. The mist originates in there and we must defeat it."

"Not much for consolation, our noble knight, is he?" Armin asked of Helimslynch as he trouped dutifully into the Frost Cavern. Still, a swift punch in the back of the knee spurred the Elven hunter forward.

"We will not die this day, Elf of Nervousness!" Helimslynch bellowed.

As the noble Trinity entered the Frost Caverns, Armin sensed that they were being watched but said nothing. It was possibly an animal nearby. As the heroes passed the crystalline stalagmites that had once been unfortunate sinners, one such stalagmite barely moved. It was just enough movement to give way to the crystalline form of a frosty humanoid.

"The temptation of sloth refuses to fell the noble heroes!" Silax mused. "However, the eternal rest of the White Death will still mark their downfall for disturbing me in my tunnels!"

Jovan took a moment to analyze a nearby stalagmite as the Fellowship pressed forward. He still could not believe the hearsay that these carefully crafted stalagmites had once been his fellow humans. He certainly could not agree with the church's notion that any person *deserved* to be condemned to the White Death. That banishment remained based on a worldly interpretation of the Sacred Text that had been voted to be agreed upon as the "correct" interpretation. No matter how "terrible" the "enemy of the cloth," did they not have a right to just punishment by a just deity? Furthermore, if by "enemy of the cloth," Mother Superior was referring to "a loud voice of protest," would it not do her spirit well to turn an even better listening ear to that voice?

"These unbelievers sinned against the cloth until their last frozen breath." A slight tenor timbre interrupted Jovan's thoughts. "It is tragic that they did not come to understand where their lives of sin would lead them until it was too late."

The Knight of Salvation had been so lost in thought that first impulse guided a single hand to the Icarus's hilt until second impulse reminded him that the archer was nearby.

"What is saddening is that a House of Believers turned to exile and murder against those whose sole offense was to speak out against its rude interpretations of a text that was designed to be sacred." Jovan observed. "A listening ear could have saved many lives from the fate surrounding us. Come; these men and women rest as they do because they have lost their abilities to move. We stand as we do because of lingering effects of the haze of sloth that led us in here. We must cut off its source."

Bourg began to unearth the Icarus from its sheath once more. Still, a consuming blast of arctic air very nearly stopped him in his movements if not for the protection of his armor. The blast had been focused directly on the Knight of Salvation. Armin and Helimslynch had detected the anomaly and each grabbed their choice weapons in case there was an unseen enemy to contend with. As the two members of the accompanying Fellowship turned to look, however, each were struck full on with the Nardot Mists at their strongest. It was clearly a final desperate attempt at failure.

"We cannot defend the Knight of Salvation as it stands. The Anon Plains will fall to the White Death next." Armin drawled, lazily dropping the bow and quiver of arrows to his side.

"We will rest in our defeat before heading back." Helimslynch yawned. "We have taken our turns at fighting Gorrenwrath; perhaps another group will fare better."

As Helimslynch's words, devoid of his natural gruff bark, filtered into Armin's thoughts, he could not believe his ears. It was one thing for Armin to give way to thoughts of weakness and allow weakness to ascend to laziness. However, that was not Helimslynch's nature!

Armin did all that he could to concentrate and he could see a crystalline humanoid hiding amidst the frozen sinners. Perhaps he was directing this arctic blast from one hand and the Nardot Mist from his other. The two separate attacks even came together at one point and formed a narrow path leading right to their crystalline oppressor. Armin hunched low to collect his bow and quiver, shook his senses back together, loaded up a select arrow, and let fly with the natural projectile. As Armin fought, the Knight of Salvation was moments away from succumbing to the White Death and Helimslynch was struggling against the debilitating laziness of lost confidence.

As the arrow flew, it naturally became weighed down by snow and ice and its tip became a sharp projectile. However, it was the sharp projectile that mattered most as the arrow still completed its journey and pierced Silax in a crystalline rib. With a high pitched yelp of pain and bewilderment, Silax shrank back from his standing position camouflaged against the cavern wall. In stumbling backward, Silax silenced the barrage of the Nardot Mist and naturally reached over to check his pierced rib. Still, the icy blast did not silence itself in time. With a cry of pain in failure, Silax became succumb to the pain of his own arctic chill and froze in place, his crystalline body shattering. Armin collapsed once more, dropping his bow and quiver clumsily beneath the effects of the lingering Nardot Mists. It was evident that, while he had collapsed to sloth in the end, he had still won a great victory for the Fellowship.

Silax was frozen beneath the very White Death that he had yielded as a weapon. In his demise, the Nardot Mist was silenced to not even descend its lazy spell over Nardot's peak. Minutes turned to hours and hours dragged on from dusk until the early dawn of the next day. Finally, the Knight of Salvation, protected by his armor, could move once more. Alongside the renewed Knight of Salvation, his allies were hazily stumbling back to their feet once more as well. The night was over, the evil defeated, and the temptation of slothfulness dispersed.

"Noble archer," Bourg declared, dropping to a single knee in humble gratitude, "we owe our continued survival this day to your efforts. You pierced Silax when I could not move and Helimslynch had given way to slothfulness."

"The vigor of Dwarven kind pulled me through for those extra moments that I required." Armin reflected. "Without your fighting spirit, friend Helimslynch, I would have been the first to fall."

"Bah; it was your Elven weakness that marked my downfall!" Helimslynch snorted. "A contagious shortcoming, it is! Enjoy your victory, Brother Elf. Your victory stopped the Nardot Mists from extending beyond Nardot's borders. It won't be freezing our crops or luring peoples beyond these mountain shores to slothfulness."

"Let us take our celebrated hero back to the Anon Plains." Bourg advised, a chuckling smile crossing his face, "I am certain that he would like to know for certain that Princess Talian has survived the night."

Armin didn't need much more inspiration to move on than that. As Helimslynch afforded a hearty chuckle at the mischievous humor, it was Armin who led the way back to the Anon Plains. After all, the Knight of Salvation knew of the nature of the Celestial Guardians and did not carry any doubts over Talian's fate. Armin, though he carried few doubts about her survival, had to recognize that the underlying concern was still there...

The Anon Plains were no worse for wear when the heroes returned, despite the arrival of the Nardot Mists. The fact that any residual destruction was nowhere in sight perplexed the Knight of Salvation for a moment.

It was Armin who discovered Talian. The celestial princess was very tired but a smile of relief still flooded over her face as she recounted a tale unasked for.

"The Ring of Renecar," she offered, "it increased my p-powers of healing. My increased healing magic even stayed off the advancing Nardot Mist enough for the steeds and the vegetation to survive."

"You have done much at the risk of your own rest." Armin applauded. "You are a goddess amongst your fellow Guardians, fairest Talian."

"Truly the celebrated powers of the Ring of Renecar are not done justice by the tales!" Helimslynch declared, "Continue to take that ring at its worth, Talian. Only then will we destroy this Gorrenwrath's evil!"

The Knight of Salvation hung back for a moment and gazed upon the Ring of Renecar adorning Talian's finger. Truly, it increased her healing powers to the point of defending the Anon Plains; there was no denying that. However, he could see the toll that using the ring had taken on her. Also, the device had been presented to her by an agent of the force that meant to destroy the Fellowship! On top of all of that, Bourg did remember reading *something* about the Ring of Renecar that continued to quietly nag at his mind.

"Do not use the power of Renecar if it can be avoided, Talian." Bourg advised, "We must know more about it before cavalierly unlocking its secrets."

Talian began to nod in understanding. Still, the voices from around her would not take such an edict so kindly.

"She has used her great powers to do what we could not alone!" Armin announced, offended on behalf of she who had taken no offense. "You are continuing to chastise her for using the Ring when it was the Ring that truly kept Anon protected! She has done well."

"Only through the Ring of Renecar can we destroy Gorrenwrath's evil!" Helimslynch spat.

"My friends," Bourg interjected, "we are each plagued by tiredness. Let **destruction** remain Gorrenwrath's way. I will settle only for his *defeat*. Talian, please do understand that I never meant to speak against you."

"I-I know." Talian reflected, the true pain and tiredness in her face masked once more by her ceremonial iron mask. She had anticipated adulations upon the heroes' return as a member of their quest who had done just as much to aid in this victory. From Helimslynch and Armin, she had received such exaltations. From the Knight of Salvation, she had received the gentlest form of a tongue-lashing.

The heroes mounted their steeds to press on their quest. As the expedition did so, Talian took to the air once more with Elion at her side and the Ring of Renecar glistening on her finger. The glistening item begged to be used once more...

ENVY

As the Son of the Cloth, Jovan Bourg, by rights, had everything. Whatever his heart desired and so much more was his for the taking. His mother was the church's most superior ruler and his father was a highly respected voice in the military serving the unbelievers. That made Jovan Bourg extremely important to both factions by definition with much political clout for a boy of his short ten years. Maxim Bourg, ever observant to what his wife's teachings were doing to his son, could sense the adverse effects of such teachings of self-importance. True to form, the father took it upon himself to engrain a degree of wisdom in his son's life. His plan took a visit to Nauros that Mother Superior would never approve and dutiful Joto would never tell her of.

The village of Nauros was collapsed in poverty and crime. Families, neighbors, and friends fell apart at the seams through arrest or illness on a nightly basis. Missionary soldiers patrolled the streets under the auspices of becoming an outlet to share the word. Those same missionaries proved just as happy making arrests instead. Children who were orphaned by the collapsing social structure of Nauros were arrested for curfew laws. Women were arrested and humiliated if they had kept an unfathered baby or, worse yet, aborted one. Adults were arrested for the crime of not having a bible. "Crimes against the church," the offenses were called, and missionaries moved through the streets unchecked. The soldiers carried more bayonets and blades than copies of the Sacred Text.

Such rampant military action only caused the soldiering forces of the unbelievers to arm themselves and march the streets against the tyranny of the Cloth. In the middle of one such battle, Maxim Bourg escorted his son through the streets with a forceful guiding hand. Jovan took in his surroundings with wide eyed curiosity as unmarked soldiers clashed. It was difficult to tell which side was fighting for whom. There was no telling who had instigated the conflict anymore. As the weather grew cold and rain began to fall, Jovan's eyes fell upon a single young girl in a heavy cloak. She stood huddled against a neighboring building. Jovan, dressed in only his church tunic, approached the girl. He was already fishing through his pockets for the obligatory payment to make the transaction a fair deal. Suddenly, he was nearly struck down by the halting hand on his shoulder.

"Where are you going, my son?" Maxim Bourg demanded, his eyes flashing warning.

"To pay her for her heavy cloak, I am cold." Jovan shivered, "You had me leave home without my cloak and she can always duck into that building behind her for warmth."

"She can go in there for warmth because she has nowhere else to go!" Bourg scolded the youth. "That is the orphanage. She has already lost her family to this rampant police state; let her keep her cloak, rotten boy!"

Before Maxim Bourg could stop him, Jovan squirmed free of his father's grip and approached the girl. Then, as the war continued unabated and the rain only picked up, Jovan Bourg slipped the girl his payment anyway. He then offered her his tunic as well. Maxim Bourg, originally ready to upbraid his son as the boy had never heard, observed him with more pride than he could remember for his generosity instead.

The Nauros of lore retained its image of downfall. Mounted soldiers still rode the streets by night. Which faction these undercover officers served first was really only settled once the troops took action. Still, for the most part, if the downtrodden remained to their homes after nightfall, they did not have to worry if the mounted riders came from the church to take them away for petty grievances. Even the riders of the unbelievers represented a threat; they would gladly strike down the missionary soldiers without caring who was caught in the crossfire. Then came the night, nearly three decades in the making, when missionary and unbelieving forces met in the square of Nauros once again. It had been long ages since the physical manifestation of the war had surfaced in the middle of the square. The first gunshot to shatter the uneasy silence made clear that old demons separating the believer and unbeliever had not been forgotten.

As shots rang out and the battle raged between the most militant voices in the divided factions, fire erupted from nearby. Flames enveloped many homes in a devastation beyond that of the war in the village square.

The inferno that had waited too long to take its reward was paving its own path of demise. Only two people remained unnoticed and unchecked to monitor the destructive path of fire.

"Gorrenwrath's path of evil has come a long way, has it not, my dear?" the hulking, dull-skinned man demanded of his raven-haired ally.

"The warmongering is a cute little manipulation of *weak* human hearts, Drax." The woman reassured him. "But my inferno is responsible for far more destruction."

"You feel threatened, my dear Mynos?" Drax demanded with a rumbling chuckle. "My war has lasted far longer."

"And my fire has *still* taken so much more of Nauros." Mynos insisted, "Nauros will still mark the hated Fellowship's final stand."

"And you're just jealous enough to try to mark their downfall yourself!" Drax grunted.

Mynos paused just long enough to remove a single glove, breathe into her hand, then settle that hand on Drax's temple and watch his eyes widen in pain just before he collapsed.

"Just powerful enough *to succeed, Drax."* Mynos reassured him, removing her hand from the demon's temple and replacing her glove. "But you can stay here and rest just in case..."

Nauros had not improved since his last visit. There was a chance that it had never since it had established its sense of poverty. It was a disturbing image of an inherited state of downfall that Jovan Bourg tried his best to get out of his head as Danavas carried him on his latest quest. Still, Jovan had to shake clear such disheartening, paralyzing thoughts. Nauros did not require tears from the Son of the very Church that represented its tormentors. The community needed the liberation of the Knight of Salvation and the Trinity required his leadership. The Knight of Salvation successfully kept his musings to himself in determination that the city be liberated. However, it was Armin who gave pause astride noble Swift just long enough to share his concerns aloud.

"It is a tragedy what plight has befallen the community of Nauros for too long." Armin observed. "These children have followed generations only to see the destruction of the former. Their children and foreigners are marked to fall to such devastation. Generations shall see the calamities that have befallen fair Nauros, just as these poor souls must observe...[4] "

Helimslynch still hadn't recovered enough of his stamina since his bout of slothfulness to speak his peace just yet. Still, he risked a fairly nasty glare for the Elven archer that caused Armin to give pause for but a moment before continuing.

"What would future generations think of this land that the Great Almighty has sent to destruction for the sins of the father? Is this land their destined inheritance?" Armin demanded, "I fear that even the Knight of Salvation and his Trinity would be hard-pressed to relieve this destruction."

"This destruction comes from the wrath of war and collapse of the downtrodden." Talian announced, swooping in alongside the archer just in time to take him to one side. "Nauros's collapse is not by the sin of the poor and impoverished who settle on its shores. This path of destruction comes from a battle that the church is just as happy to take up arms in as the unbeliever."

"Indeed, winged one." Jovan observed. "To gaze upon the downfall of Nauros is to imagine what would happen to all of Mother Trina if this warring from both sides remains unchecked."

"Take up the Ring of Renecar, beautiful Talian," Armin declared, "and your mighty WarCleaver, Helimslynch. Gorrenwrath shall make his final stand on Trina before his manipulations of war can reach other worlds beyond our shores."

"It will not be enough, dutiful archer." Jovan observed with a sad of shake of his head that moved his helmet. With that, he paused Danavas and turned to face his accompanying Fellowship. "Gorrenwrath is but the principal manipulator of the outcome of a war of ages. It is preju-dice, suspicion, and hatred that govern the battle between believers and unbelievers. These are sad states of the human condition that must be remedied in due time. Onward, noble Fellowship. The shores of Nauros have awaited their salvation from poverty for too long."

Jovan turned Danavas once more to face their destination and coaxed his steed into a trot once more. After a moment's rest while the Knight's words sank in, Helimslynch and Armin followed in his footsteps. Before long, Talian flew up alongside the White Knight of Salvation.

"Do you recall anything about the Ring?" she asked.

"The words are few in the Sacred Text about items of sorcery." Bourg afforded a quip, "I fear that what it does say about sorcery is not too kind."

"True enough." Talian chuckled, "My powers of foresight should be able to decipher the mystery but they are still silenced."

"I still advise to only awaken that ring's true potential when absolutely necessary until we know the mystery behind its origins." Jovan announced. "I hope that you understand."

"I understand." Talian conceded, her eyes faced just ahead beneath her ceremonial mask. "I suggest that if we came here to cleanse Nauros, we best start now while there is a community left to save."

Jovan and the others glanced ahead to see what Talian had seen and all froze right where they sat. The smoke from the raging inferno continuously stung at their eyes. Through that smoke, they could still make out the sights and sounds of the battle in village square. That day, as every day, the believers proved quite willing to participate in the same fight as the unbelievers. The differences governing their divisions were no longer evident.

"Talian, fend off that blaze; use the Ring if you have to." Jovan declared. "Armin, separate those two bloodthirsty factions away from one another and try to talk good sense into the believers. Helimslynch, try to talk peace into the unbelieving factions. I will aid everyone as best as I can. Today marks the day when Nauros must rise up to be a better place for the downtrodden."

Instantly, the Fellowship sprang into action once more. As the heroes separated to contend with the warring factions and with the blaze, they were unaware of the sinister agents watching their movements and manipulating the continued collapse of Nauros. Mynos monitored the Knight of Salvation's movements hungrily as he approached the blaze. Drax could just as easily continue to manipulate a war that he had started; the Knight was to be her prize. Then, the enchantress's eyes settled on Talian and narrowed in jealousy.

"The Knight of Salvation must be *mine* to control! I cannot have him following another." she exclaimed, snapping her fingers and raising Drax from his stupor. "My dear Drax, I raise you once more to delay the Elf and Dwarf. Talian's life will be forfeit by my hands, making the the good Knight mine. You may go, profane puppet."

The lumbering demon clambered mechanically back to his feet as if just relearning the use of his limbs.

"Distract the Fellowship from their task." Drax droned, oblivious to a small green light pulsating above his temple where Mynos's hand had touched. "Your will shall be done, my queen."

Mynos chuckled viciously to herself as the man who was once her major competition for Gorrenwrath's favor now marched off to heed her commands with ease. Once Talian's interference would no longer prove a bother, Mynos could easily allure the White Knight of Salvation to her vile affections as well. That could take some time, but the result when the White Knight slew Gorrenwrath on *her* behalf would be more than worth the wait. All that the enchantress of envy could do was to bide her time. Such was a task that she normally hated but the results could only bear pleasure for her. The raven haired beauty drew up the hood of her dark cloak, observed the effects of her inferno one more time, and withdrew into the darkness to await those who meant to fight the flames.

Despite the length of time that the blazing inferno had already accumulated, it was burning at its worst by the time that Talian and the Knight of Salvation arrived. The blaze overtook everything that did not already belong to the destruction of war. Even the Celestial Guardian hadn't known what to expect and certainly was not prepared for the sight of the destruction that had extended over Nauros. Bourg was forced to observe the destruction at close up as well. As the image settled over him, a tear welled up in his eye, obscured from view by his helmet.

"These people's homes!" Talian cried. "This is Nauros; its people will have nowhere else to go!"

"I know." Jovan barely managed above a baritone whisper, "Y-Use the ring. Your increased power stands the best chance of fending b-back these flames."

Somehow in his weakened state, the Knight managed to unsheathe Icarus and utilized the family heirloom to unearth a large trench to quell the fires. Talian, from her renewed place in the air, aimed her hands and channeled her mystic powers. Obediently, the Ring of Renecar served to unearth an unexpected burst of magic. Still, the supercharged spell was serving its purpose well and Talian beamed with pride beneath her mask. As the Knight of Salvation firmly focused on his half of the task, only Elion could sense the plight of his mistress so long as she utilized the ring. Talian, however, remained oblivious to Elion's warnings in her latest state. Here, her powers were amplified a thousand fold and so much power was not easy to give up kindly while it still resonated.

From his place on the ground, Bourg was well aware of the power that Talian displayed. In many ways, it overshadowed an illusion of power reserved only for the true Knight of Salvation. However, such feelings could be dealt with in time. At the moment, while Talian flew through the air using magic against the flames, Bourg was trudging forward, utilizing manual labor to fend back the destruction.

Even for as much as Bourg was trying to hold his resentment in check, Mynos had already sensed the anomaly from her place nearby. The conniving enchantress promptly removed one of her gloves. The bare hand revealed crooked nails, a serpentine ring, and a barely visible green glow waiting to infect the next victim to Mynos's mental control. The enchantress kept her hood in place and ducked out of her hiding place to be right behind the Knight of Salvation. Once in reaching distance, she reached out with a single hand...

Jovan sensed the movement behind him and whipped around, shouldering the Icarus in preparation to attack. His sense of was vigor renewed by the realization that his work would not amount up to much. The Knight of Salvation's eyes flamed beneath his helmet and his weapon was poised, ready to strike an invisible attacker. As a cloaked villager shrank back in terror, Jovan grappled with the Icarus and sheathed the weapon once more. With the blade sheathed safely away, Bourg extended a hand and hoisted the terrified stranger to her feet.

"My humblest apologies; you had ...startled me." Bourg murmured, dusting off the cloak with an iron gauntlet that protected him from direct physical contact. "What are you doing out of home amidst this blaze?"

"Forgive *me*, most humble Knight of Salvation. I had to meet you for myself." Mynos purred, "You have done much for Nauros and to shoulder all of Trina's sins. Yet, a Ring of such great power rests on the hands of a *lesser* member of our beloved Fellowship?"

"There exists no *lesser* member of the Fellowship; the Knight of Salvation, the Trinity, and our allies must work in accordance." Bourg observed, struggling for the first time to believe the words himself. "Thank you for your dedication to all that we do. Please, return to your home where you are safe."

From beneath the hood of her cloak, Mynos drew her lips back in a sickly sneer.

"Of course, noblest Knight." She leered, the venom in her voice unmistakable as she observed the effects of Talian's power and formed another idea. "My home is simply over there..."

With an encompassing gesture, Mynos indicated a vacant building in the same section as Talian was continuing to work. Almost instantly, the flames caught hold of the vacant building identified as her home. It was such ferocity that the destruction was not going to hold back.

"My home!" Mynos wept, collapsing back into Bourg's waiting arms.

Bourg raised his head to summon Talian to what had happened but she already knew. A concussive burst of mystic energy echoed through the air, focused on the instant inferno. As the mystic energy swept over the blaze, the fire did die. What happened next, however, was inevitable.

As the flames dissipated to nonexistence, the building collapsed to Talian's horror, Bourg's chagrin, and Mynos's barely contained satisfaction.

The only option left for Bourg was to fling Mynos to safety and shield her from the view of the destruction. In the evidence of the collapse, Talian landed once more, the collapsing building beyond her power's ability to stop.

The damage was already done. The Celestial Guardian landed alongside the young woman and promptly removed her mask to reveal the pain that she felt upon the accidental blast. The winged Guardian opened her mouth to be the first to speak as the Ring of Renecar glowed. Still, Mynos threw back her hood, revealing eyes of venom and the desire to speak first.

"You!" she seethed, aiming a crooked nail at Talian. "You destroyed my family's home and the fire remains unchecked!"

"Her powers have done what they can to weaken the destruction. In time, a trench will quell what remains of the flames." Bourg announced, unhanding Mynos to reach for his blade.

As the Knight of Salvation began his work toiling a giant trench to suppress the blaze once more, however, Mynos turned her attention to face Talian. The Celestial Guardian was unprotected from her wrath, save for Elion.

"Vile witch!" Mynos shrieked, lunging at Talian. "You were given the Ring of Renecar, a power that should be the Knight of Salvation's! You journey with the Knight of Salvation who should rightfully be allied with *me*!"

First impulse directed Talian to fly away from the attacker. If anything else, she could use the tether to keep the enemy at bay. Still, as the Ring of Renecar glistened on her finger, she got a very different idea and launched another burst of highly destructive mystic energy. Such a spell was only intercepted and reflected harmlessly by the Icarus Blade.

"Remove the ring, Talian." Bourg demanded, "Truly it has corrupted your mind."

"The Ring is MINE!" Talian snarled as the mystic bolts of energy went around her without harming her and she approached the White Knight. "You are heralded the Son of the Cloth and championed the Knight of Salvation! Any efforts to halt Gorrenwrath's plague will only be attributed back to you! Let *me*, a rightful Celestial Guardian, keep my powers as only a member of the Trinity."

"You were given those powers to *protect* and to *heal*." Bourg chided her. "I must take Mynos to safety before you attack one another once more. Your great powers have done well in halting this destructive inferno. I ask that you continue to use them if only to silence it."

Talian reeled at the thought of continuing to accept orders from a mere human, "Son of the Church" or no. She was the Celestial Guardian who had been entrusted by the Great Savior with such great power. She had been the one who had very nearly fended off Gorrenwrath *alone* with .1% of the power that she had now! Yet, it would still be the Knight of Salvation and his precious Icarus who would receive the credit for Trina's salvation. Furthermore, Bourg still considered it his place to advise her about using an item that had been gifted to her, not he. She was expected to believe that the Ring of Renecar had more potential to do harm than a giant sword!

"Your sense of envy reflects poorly on your judgment, Son of the Cloth!" Talian murmured, only vaguely aware that her voice no longer sounded like its own. As she took to the air once more to complete her task, Elion followed Jovan Bourg and Mynos. Talian could only take in the sight of her ally following another. With that, she reared back her hands and thrust forward her mystic energy to drive back the remains of the flames alone.

Bourg carried the weakened Mynos through the streets of Nauros in search of safety, holding his dislodged helmet under one arm. From her newfound place in his armored arms, Mynos saw her chance and cradled a single hand against the Knight of Salvation.

"How unjust," Mynos pouted, "that a simple member of the Trinity should bear the Ring of Renecar and its power. She has misused its authority to destroy people's homes. Such a ring should rightfully be yours to control."

Mynos's hand glistened with energy as if to do its job. Yet, she couldn't detect any change in Bourg's demeanor as her hand settled coyly against his temple.

"It was Talian who was gifted with the ring because the ring amplifies the power of magic." Bourg explained. "Without the protection and guidance of Talian, Armin, and Helimslynch, I would have fallen from this path long ago. I would thank Trina for remembering each member of this Fellowship with credit on the day of her liberation."

As Bourg spoke, Mynos's eyes flared with envy once more. She could not take the mind of the Knight of Salvation. Without the White Knight as her servant, Gorrenwrath's defeat would gain her nothing!

"You do not desire the use of the Ring of Renecar?" Mynos demanded, squirming in her cradled position and falling back to her feet in front of her rescuer. The physical and mental contact was broken.

"I would have simply no use for the Ring even if I did know what its origins truly were." Bourg explained, settling a pair of comforting hands on the woman's shoulders. "Though you have seen your home destroyed, you try to plague my conscience with resentment of my allies. Why is this?"

As Bourg settled his hands on the woman's shoulders, the crucifix around his neck dislodged itself from beneath his armor and revealed itself in the glistening moonlight. The sight of the crucifix prompted a yelp from Mynos and she collapsed out of the startled Knight's reach. As the enchantress collapsed, Bourg lunged to help her but froze at the last minute. From her place on the ground, Mynos's hands were giving way to dust in the middle of Nauros. Stunned by such a sudden occurrence, Bourg shrank back, replaced his helmet, and reached for the Icarus once more.

"What has happened?" Bourg demanded. "Are you well?"

Mynos wouldn't answer him directly. However, her forthcoming shrieking plea gave all of the answer that Bourg required to explain the sudden ailments.

"I haven't failed!" she shrieked to no one in particular. "There is still time for but one more chance, my Lord!"

It was too late for her pleas to do any good. Her hands, arms, feet, legs, eyes, and face each gave way to dust. All at once, Bourg understood what had happened. The humanoid dust form crawled toward him to make one final attempt at filling his conscience with selfish desire and resentment.

Nevertheless, Bourg whirled the Icarus that it could catch the glistening moonlight just right yet again and weaken the wicked creation to defeat.

Mynos had been nothing, save for another agent of sinister Gorrenwrath. This enchantress had certainly come the closest to succeeding. Bourg took another moment to gather his bearings in the middle of the community of Nauros and realized that without the aid of the Fellowship, he indeed *would have* failed. Even if he had not fallen long before, then certainly the latest leg of his journey would have marked his collapse. Bourg made a silent vow that resentment would never contaminate his spirit again and replaced the Icarus in its hilt before going on his way. He had to find Talian and aid Helimslynch and Armin in their trials. Mynos was defeated and the fires extinguished. Of course, that did leave the battle between religious and unreligious that ruined Nauros more than poverty had already done. Such a battle had gone unabated for too long.

WRATH

Anger, whether righteous or no, was the principal instigator of the conflict that had torn Trina apart for too long. Whether or not the church had stepped out of line in its mission of ministry or the unbelievers were willing to listen were just sad excuses to escalate generations old anger to the fruition of bloodshed. By the age of ten, certainly the son of Maxim and Martilla Bourg had heard every excuse for the continuing bloodshed. He also realized that there was only one critical cause of the warfare.

Standing in the middle of Nauros as the fighting continued without falter piqued a long list of interesting questions in Jovan Bourg's mind. This fight was between the religious and unreligious. Why did it need to burden Nauros, a community innocent of fault in the struggle between the two factions and which already struggled with deficiency? Surely a war-torn village square was not about to deliver prosperity to the citizenry. No; this type of anger only bred violence, and such violence could only lead to destruction. Such an unfortunate outcome was certainly not limited to Nauros, but it was where it was most evident. How could two separate sides, each claiming to care so much about the well-being of the commoner, not understand that they were destroying the community? Jovan Bourg turned his head to present such a question to his father. Still, before the youth could get in a word edgewise, two rivaling soldiers had already spied the two and approached them.

"General Bourg!" Ramin Heed greeted his General, complete with a salute as if the boy were not there with them. "We have captured some of the invading forces and freed their captives. We await further instructions regarding our prisoners."

Bourg began to respond but Viscar Halas, a young missionary soldier, saw the younger Bourg and replied that much faster.

"Jovan!" he cried, "The unbelievers have stolen you right out from under Mother Superior's nose?"

*"The boy's **father** has stolen no one!" Maxim Bourg defended; then, to Heed before the question could be repeated. "Release your prisoners back to their church steeples."*

"General--" Heed insisted.

"If this fighting is to cease, one of us must lead the example." Bourg interjected. "You have freed the citizens from false arrest. I ask you again to release our prisoners. I did not come here to be in command and my son has witnessed too much of the destruction of this warfare."

The two soldiers appeared taken aback by the barbed words of the well-known general but both saluted hastily and went on their ways. As the two rival factions performed the exchange of military prisoners, Bourg shook his head sadly, took his son by a shoulder, and walked away.

Armin fired off one last arrow in his arsenal in hopes of adding to the barrier as opposed to hitting an agent of war. As usual, the archer's aim was spot on and a small barrier of arrows now formed a fence between the warring factions. It wasn't much and any rider could easily dismount, weave through the fence, and press the attack. Still, such would be a declaration of the continuation of war. This was meant to be a test between the two groups. Whoever breached the perimeter first would surely be instigating the conflict. The soldiers of the cloth merely kept their weapons close at hand and waited under the watchful eye of Armin. In their waiting, the missionaries did raise their Sacred Texts. Such could be a sign of certain unity if the Word was to be shared aloud. Armin's sharp Elven ears were tuned to listen for a delivery of the Word that the believers so hoped that the unbelievers would understand. The missionaries, in turn, read silently to themselves of a Sacred Text that they already believed in.

Helimslynch squatted alongside the riders of the unreligious, gnawng greedily on a turkey leg that one of the soldiers had fetched for the Dwarven weaponsmith. Helimslynch was no fool and knew what the peace offering of the tasty morsel was supposed to mean. However, he would not raise his WarCleaver in defense of the unreligious. Deep in the General's heart, he knew that the war had gone on for too long. Armin had done his job of using his arrows to form the simple gate that separated the two factions while watching the missionaries. Helismlynch had to do his part and keep the unreligious from fighting as well. Beneath the moonlight of Nauros,

Helimslynch glanced up and across the way to where the riders of the religious remained seated. They almost challenged the unreligious soldiers to make the first move and escalate the fighting. Still, as the Dwarven General glanced up to make eye contact with his ally, Armin was busily collecting his bow, arrows, and blades. He then whispered to Viscar Halas and betrayed his post to slink off into the obscurity of night. The missionary soldiers were left under the care of their prized military leader. As Armin slipped away into the night with his weapons, the believers were left to their own druthers unsupervised. The unbelievers raised their murmurs of suspicion to one another and raised their weapons, anticipating an ambush. After a moment's thought, Helimslynch raised the WarCleaver as well before beckoning at the unbelievers that they would not make the first move. Nonethless, he risked a glare across the way that he anticipated the first move from the believers in the name of religious oppression. At the moment, Helimslynch's loyalty was to the faction of unbelievers. There was no telling why Armin had left his post but Helimslynch wasn't prepared to take any chances.

While he could have sworn that he had sensed something in the woods worth investigating, Armin still felt like a fool for having trusted the missionaries outside of his supervision. Though the church tried its best to bury the evidence of the actions that their "missionaries" took while on undertakings in Nauros, there were certain actions that polite society could not ignore. For the church's actions in Nauros, even the most loyal of believers with the capacity to think for themselves condemned the military actions committed. These were brave men and women who were supposed to be performing *missionary* work! Many of these atrocities had been field-commandeered by Viscar Halas. Yet, here was Halas being trusted to babysit his bloodthirsty forces. However, Armin swore that he had detected something moving just beyond the field of vision of the village square and the hunter had a job to do. Praying that none of the riders would try anything foolish, Armin took up his position where he could casually observe his forces but also see beyond the village square. From his new post, the archer leveled his bow across a shoulder and waited.

Cloaked in the shadows between two buildings roughly one hundred yards away, Drax could see that the fighting had come to a tense standstill. The Herculean demon certainly had the brute force to lunge into the middle of the fray and effectively destroy all of the soldiers. Still, that was not what he was sent to do. For all of the demon god's musculature, he still had a degree of cunning that he needed to utilize. Drax gazed down upon an iron throwing-axe by his left hand and a spear, almost in the shape of an arrow, by his right. Furthermore, as clouds gathered to unleash their anger over the anxious military factions, Drax could see the Elven archer while his dull grey body was still cloaked in enough shadows that even his opponent hadn't seen an enemy yet. Gorrenwrath's latest agent chuckled deeply and thrust the spear with a mighty hand, aimed momentarily right at the archer. He would see no choice but to react.

Armin saw the oncoming projectile, loaded up his bow and drew back the string. As the first clap of enraged thunder rocked Nauros, he launched an arrow just as the projectile that had been heading straight for him banked off of a building and out into the village square...

The sudden clap of thunder would have normally startled the two uneasy armies back into battle. The crack of thunder in this instance might as well have been a whisper compared to the twine of a nearby bowstring moments after the Elf had vanished. Almost instantly, an arrow arced out from behind the buildings. The projectile sailed right over the heads of the believers and struck down an unbeliever right in his unarmored throat with precision accuracy.

The gasps and murmurs of confusion from the missionaries were only overpowered by the protests of betrayal and cries of bloodshed from the unbelievers. From his place alongside the unbelievers, Helimslynch grumbled a curse and his eyes flared for bloodlust as he prepped WarCleaver with his throwing arm. Armin had just betrayed the Fellowship; no, everyone who had trusted him. No, he had betrayed *all of Trina* through his cowardly acts! The Elf had provoked the fight's continuation. It was the Dwarf who wanted revenge as his arm came forward to release WarCleaver...

As Helimslynch's throwing arm reached its arc, a large steel axe flew forward with precision accuracy and slashed Halas's steed through the throat with gut wrenching impact. The believers silenced their protests that they had never understood what had happened before and raised their weapons upon seeing a noble animal struck down by a member of the Fellowship. The unbelievers were only upset that a mere animal had fallen and, their weapons already in hand, were waiting to oblige their religious oppressors. The fact that Helimslynch was staring perplexedly at WarCleaver, still in his own hand, was left ignored by either side. The giant iron blade soaring in between the two factions, however, could not be ignored and the rivaling armies reflexively backed away...

Icarus settled itself into the ground and caught the light of an oncoming flash of lightning to give way back to a glimmering cross of hope. Viscar Halas, crawling out from under his noble steed and forcing his way back to his feet, beckoned to his soldiers to wait as they each shrank back from the debilitating glow. Helimslynch, seeing Halas make the first move and knowing who was coming through the village square, raised his axe in evidence to the missionaries that he had never thrown it. He then barked at his own troops to wait. It wasn't moments later that the Knight of Salvation approached the Icarus and collected the blade from its perch. Talian, in turn, placed a mystic barrier between the two rivaling factions.

"Jovan, you've returned!" Halas exclaimed, beckoning to his fellow soldiers to dismount and managing to kneel down with two bad legs in honor of the arrival of the Son of the Cloth. As the Son of the Church approached from afar, the unbelievers murmured ruthlessly to one another. Their murmurs only got louder as the Icarus was raised from the ground back to its master's hand. The protests were promptly silenced when the sword was sheathed safely away. The gut reactions from both sides had been for Jovan Bourg, the Son of the Cloth, and the Son of the Church. However, no one gathered had anything to say to the Knight of Salvation.

"People of Trina, this violence has gone on unchecked for too long." Bourg observed, watching as Armin rejoined his allies from afar. "Nauros is blameless in your historic struggles. Yet, a community that is already poverty stricken must face the ultimate costs of your violent hatred of one another."

"The church does not recognize violent hatred as one of its practices, Jovan." Halas protested the insinuation, struggling sheepishly to recover his footing. Still, the Knight of Salvation settled a hand on his shoulder and hoisted Halas back to his feet. He then signaled Danavas to carry the injured general away for urgent care.

"I am certain that if the church did recognize violent hatred when it saw it, it would heed my constant warnings to take another look at the Sacred Text and retest its line of interpretation." Jovan declared, his humble baritone refusing to unleash a note of disdain.

"The unwashed struck down a noble animal." Xian Imor, the youngest of the missionaries, insisted. "All that we've ever done is come to expand the understanding of the church!"

"Then I ask you again to leave the stables with fewer weapons and more copies of the Sacred Text." Bourg insisted. "The believers did not strike first and the unbelievers raised no hand in vengeance. Talian and her faithful companion, Elion, saw everything from the air. You've all been misled."

"The archer fired upon us, White Knight!" Pelos Lascar announced. "He *murdered* my brother. We all saw his arrow!"

Helimslynch approached the fallen soldier and bent down to inspect the body. Triumphantly he raised the projectile for evidence, even if for his own eyes, against the archer. Here was the man who consistently referred to him as brother and then betrayed Trina! Armin, still keeping his distance from a crowd of believers who were just as angry with him as the unbelievers, paused to wait as Helimslynch palmed the projectile, inspecting it up close and turning it over in his hands for closer examination before addressing the unbelievers once more, his evidence still in hand.

"We saw a **spear**." Helimslynch observed with a chuckle. "Armin is as innocent of blame for this offense as I."

"Each of our ancestors has spent too long destroying an innocent town through our need for bloodshed." Bourg concluded. "Now, the Fellowship will stay here personally to help you each rebuild the community that this constant fighting has destroyed."

The believers and unbelievers found common ground just then. The Knight of Salvation had made a good point. This was their war, not Nauros's. Additionally, what the soldiers had destroyed in the already underprivileged community, they could certainly help to rebuild. When the mystic barrier separating the two armies dissipated, Armin paired off with Helimslynch in repairing a few buildings near the village square. From there, believers and unbelievers paired one another off in repairing damaged buildings or ministering to the needy people through food and drink or sharing of the Sacred Text. It was the most heartfelt sense of community to ever discover the shores of Nauros and it could only be interrupted by one thing.

A loud roar erupted from near the square, yelling over the remaining crashes of thunder. The abrupt sound sent the displaced citizens scrambling for cover and the soldiers after their armaments once more. They were not one another's enemies at the moment. They both had to band together against something much worse. As Armin heard that bestial roar, he mouthed something to himself and reached not for his bow and arrows but his underutilized twin blades.

A dull gray creature, almost humanoid in stature except for his gargantuan height, Herculean muscles, and the color of his skin, marched into Nauros Square. With one hand, the demon was wrenching unsuccessfully at an arrow in its chest. Two things were certain at that moment: this demon was a creature of Gorrenwrath and he was already injured. Impulsively, the soldiers of belief and disbelief each readied their spears and arrows. Still, Drax paused once more out of range of any archer save for Armin.

"I was here to destroy Nauros through war as but the first city to actually collapse beneath Gorrenwrath's dominion." Drax rumbled, barely able to stand through the agony of the arrow lodged in his rib. "However, if Nauros refuses to collapse under the wickedness of war, it will just have to fall under other means."

Without warning, Drax reared back his bald head, then thrust forward once more. Instantly, a bolt of destructive energy emanated from the creature's eyes, destroying all that had been previously reconstructed. The sudden blast certainly kept the soldiers at bay before they would ever try to defend the city.

Only the White Knight of Salvation finally developed a plan as the beams of destruction swept over Nauros, the angry crashes of thunder providing an appropriate backdrop for the rage that would be the downfall of Nauros. Bourg beckoned that the soldiers get behind him for safety. The mere riders ducked for cover without argument, leaving Armin and Helimslynch standing stubbornly at the Knight's side to aide him and Talian flying overhead.

As the destructive beams arced toward Bourg, it was the final push that almost caused even the Trinity to obligingly shrink back as they had been asked to do. However, such destruction would never touch the Knight of Salvation. Swiftly, as if gaining stamina, the Knight of Salvation raised the Icarus once more as if preparing to drive the blade home. However, as had happened so many times, the family heirloom was not utilized as a weapon of war. Jovan turned the weapon on its side and reflected the beams of energy right back at their source, blinding and disorienting the enemy momentarily. Drax now had one injured rib and had lost his sight. Now was the opportune moment to drive the point home.

"Utilize the Icarus, Jovan Bourg!" Lascar declared, "Make your father proud!"

"I intend to make Trina proud." Jovan replied, sheathing the Icarus once more. "Talian, the creature is momentarily stunned and easily con-fused. Draw him from here."

Talian nodded, flapped her mighty wings, and soared at the injured, disoriented Drax. As the Celestial Guardian dove, Drax clawed violently at air with his free hand as he half occupied himself with exorcising the arrow from his rib. Still, he succeeded in neither and Talian doubled around the demon before flying backwards and, therefore, out of range. As the demon lumbered clumsily after his prey, there came the sound of a sickening slash and the leg opposite the creature's bruised rib collapsed. There was a moment where no one could explain what had happened. Then Helimslynch approached the pitiful demon and loosed the now bloodied WarCleaver from the creature's leg with pride. He then unearthed the arrow from its rib to allow the wound to continue to bleed. With that done, the Dwarven General nodded in satisfaction of what he had done and slung WarCleaver across his back once more. Finally, he tossed the arrow carelessly back to Armin. As the stout general approached the Fellowship once more, he expected adulations. As Talian returned to the Fellowship's side and not one of them had anything to say, Helimslynch decided that he was in for a long wait.

The pathetic creature remained in the middle of Nauros Square as the clouds continued to unleash their fury over the community. All of the while, the soldiers under the tutelages of Armin and Talian did all that they could to gather medical supplies in case the need should arise. Drax was an enemy and an agent of Gorrenwrath, but he was still a living being. Besides, slaying the creature would be in direct correlation to an act of anger. Acts of anger had been what had turned prejudice and suspicion into acts of war in the middle of Nauros for too long. Besides, using such aggression on Drax, the demon of wrath, would surely only feed Gorrenwrath more power. It would take an act of mercy to sap both the agent and its master of their powers.

As the heroes gathered materials, however, the sky became dark once more as if another violent rage was threatening to disrupt sunup. For all of the explanations that the heroes were trying to come up with for the sudden shift, Drax could only sense one. The wounded demon managed to turn his eyes to the oncoming clouds above him.

"No..." Drax whimpered.

Within moments, a single lightning bolt erupted from the sky and found its target in the failed demon soldier. Gorrenwrath had clearly already known of the failure by his latest agent and was none too pleased with such an outcome. As suddenly as the storm had threatened Nauros with its rage, it passed over, having found and punished its victim.

Sunup graced Nauros with its presence unabated and the soldiers were still hard at work restoring the community. Bourg took a few extra minutes to watch the work being done on the buildings or the ministry being performed between religious and unreligious and soldier and eager citizen. Concealed beneath his helmet, a tear of hope for Trina's future welled up in the Knight of Salvation's eye as he waited for faithful Danavas to return. The Fellowship needed to continue on its quest.

Elion's arrival interrupted Bourg's thoughts and the horned falcon screeched at Talian for a few moments before allowing her to translate. Her face was crestfallen before she could speak.

"Jovan," she announced, "the next siting of the most Evil has been identified. It is Krill."

Bourg took that bit of news as one would a punch in the gut. Still, he squared his shoulders determinedly and allowed the piece of news to wash right over him. The site of great darkness and Evil was the site of the highest church.

Instantly, Danavas rejoined the other steeds of the Fellowship, having dropped off Viscar Halas for medical care. As the horse approached its rider, it seemed to have a sense for something that it wasn't sure that its rider knew just yet. As the steed trotted up to the Knight of Salvation, however, Bourg situated himself in the steed's saddle and turned to face the Trinity.

"We must leave the troops to their rebuilding and Nauros to its dru-thers." He announced. "This place has been exorcised of Gorrenwrath's disciples. My home, however, has not. Onward, noble Fellowship."

Without another word on the matter, the Fellowship set out on its next quest, knowing very well how painful the destination would have to be for Jovan Bourg. However, the Knight of Salvation could not afford to dwell on such weakness as he led the way out of Nauros's gates.

PRIDE

The sound of iron against iron rang like a beckon call from the village square of Krill for anyone who was anyone to drop what they were doing and witness the fights. The boys utilized Krill Square for combat. Sometimes these battles were to settle disputes. Sometimes they were just for the sport of it. Often times, even the combatants didn't know why they were fighting. Always, the reasoning involved pride. As for the two combatants at the moment, it was very much over disputes. Between these two boys, there was barely enough room once the crowd formed for all of the victor's coveted pride.

Eighteen year old Demetrius Slade was the bigger and stronger of the two combatants and wouldn't let sixteen year old Jovan Bourg forget about the handicap. Before their peers, mostly male but with one or two females thrown in to celebrate whichever boy won, Demetrius garnered extra vigor in combat. He drove the point of his lance straight at his younger, smaller, and less physically imposing opponent. Rumor had had it that Slade's girlfriend had been making time with the Son of the Cloth and then the two had bumped each other in the hallway that morning. Still, everyone knew that that was a poorly conceived excuse to throw a grudge match.

Bourg was backed into a corner. Slade was ready to deliver the final humbling blow that would siphon any of the Son of the Cloth's sense of pride for the duration of the academic year. Still, being taller and stronger made Slade somewhat clumsier as well. It was a small advantage but Bourg needed to take it.

Bourg used an armored foot to throw Slade off of balance. It was a somewhat cheap shot but Slade would have gladly done worse to him. The underhanded maneuver worked out and drove Slade off course long enough for Bourg to step out of the corner and circle his opponent, waiting for the older boy to restore his weapon and his balance. What happened instead was a gauntleted uppercut to Bourg's face that bloodied his lip and dislocated his nose as his smirking opponent picked up his weapon. The crowd response was a mixture of jeering the underhanded move and cheering the ongoing rivalry between the two boys.

"It stings, right, Son of Church Linen?" Demetrius demanded. "We all know that mommy's the church's top wretch and your father's marching for the unbelievers. How exactly did they come up with you again?"

The crowd joined in the jeering for but a moment; then the echoing of a steel lance against an iron helmet caused them to swallow the mockery. Demetrius was struck in the head and went down flat on his back, his ears sharply ringing from the blow against the side of his helmet. As the taller boy struggled to regain his weapon and his composure, an iron boot came down on top of his gauntleted hand, pinning it in place.

"Big tree fall hard." The bloody faced boy announced, prepping his lance for one final humbling blow.

The final blow never occurred. A much older hand seized the lance, snapped it in two, and Maxim Bourg marched his son home to the hilarity of his peers, announcing that the fight was already over…

As dawn broke over Krill, Martilla Bourg seemed rather proud as she drew open the shades of her mansion on the window-side facing her church. The direct attacks against the church by unwashed civilian soldiers had been stayed off by patriots supporting everything that the cloth stood for. Not only were the church's patrons protecting the church from undue assault at home, they were working abroad in the unwashed, unfortunate sector of Nauros as well.

"Any business this morning, Mister Joto?" Mother Superior called down the steps, descending the mansion stairs into the spacious dining room. Breakfast was already waiting for her arrival. Dutifully standing alongside the staircase was Joto, smiling pleasantly at his Mother Superior.

"No, my lady." Joto announced. "Halas is being well attended inside the church after last night's injuries and the Fellowship is returning home for a brief visit."

"And which of these unkempt souls intentionally harmed one of our missionaries?" Mother Superior demanded, settling into a chair and sipping her tea.

Joto drew in a fine breath on his way out the door to attend to the church grounds.

"Injury is but a minor existing condition in warfare, Mother Superior." Joto replied. "I shall prepare the church for the Knight of Salvation's arrival."

"Let us prepare the stables and he'll be satisfied." Mother Superior retorted.

She was waiting for Joto to laugh with his mistress at the joke, he knew. She would be in for a long wait. To use the stables instead of the house proper took an appropriate degree of humility that the father had taught the son and the mother would never understand.

"Of course, Mother Superior." Joto replied, closing the door behind him to set off on his daily tasks...

The sun shone self-importantly over all of Krill, gracing the city with its glowing beauty. The blonde gargantuan man of thirty-seven years rose from slumber and fastened on a dark armor that, if not for the black color, would have matched the Knight of Salvation's. Then, wordlessly, the man raised a mighty blade. His eyes, greying over the years, flashed a sense of hatred where youthful determination once was. Demetrius Slade had been bested by Jovan Bourg too many times. The White Knight of Salvation had yet to cross blades with the Black Knight...

The path separating the impoverished village of Nauros from the privileged city of Krill was as far in miles as it was in understanding of cultures. Still, the White Knight of Salvation weathered the journey astride his noble charger and backed by the efforts of the Trinity on his arduous quest. The thought of his homestead and the church capital being a harbor for such temptation as to prompt evil was a disheartening notion. Without the aid of the Fellowship, Jovan Bourg would have surrendered the mantle of Knight of Salvation to the next unsuspecting soul without a moment's thought. Bourg's disappointment in the moral failures of his own homeport could be dealt with in due time. Sitting astride Danavas, Bourg had folded open his copy of the family's Sacred Text and stumbled directly to the following passage; one of the few passages that spoke directly of the Trinity:

For the Trinity if it should work reasonably
Should hold but THREE persons
To work with two or four is not a proper Trinity
And failure is its destiny.

The destiny of a Trinity of four was *failure*. Jovan could argue all that he wanted that the Knight of Salvation was part of the *Fellowship*, only backed by the *Trinity*. But were not the Trinity and Fellowship one in the same? Had the Knight of Salvation, sworn to carry the mantle of Trina's freedom, ensured its demise instead?

The harsh, grating bark of a speaker that the Knight of Salvation could not yet see took him out of his thoughts of anticipated failure.

"So this is where the pretty people go to worship their Grandiose King?" Helimslynch snorted. "What'll they say when they meet their maker face-to-face, Son of Filthy Church Linen?"

"Mother Superior often speaks recommendation of the articles of repentance between the confidences of worshippers and their revered Mother Superior." Bourg reflected. "It would perhaps benefit her and the church elders to remember such a common practice when they must meet the judgment of a far Greater King."

"You don't speak much as a defender of the church, Jovan Bourg." Armin observed.

"I do not ride here to defend the church. I have come to defend Trina in all of its members." Bourg insisted before pausing in the middle of the path and turning Danavas to face the Trinity once more. "This is Krill; it serves not only as Trina's religious capital in the wake of the downfall of Mount Lyr but it is my home. Yet, its descent into temptation has marked it as a place to be exorcised of Evil. Is that the very church that you suggest that I defend more valiantly, noble Armin?"

Armin considered such a question, then shook his head, adjusting his bow against Swift's iron saddle.

"Loyal Helimslynch," Bourg continued, "you speak of the church and its fellows as though they have mastered the language of braggarts. It may be true that the early church wrote the language of boasting of a Creator that only they believed in. Yet, such boastful tongues were only *perfected* when adopted by believers and unbelievers in equal parts."

Helimslynch considered what was said for a moment and wanted to refute such chiding with a haughty chuckle. Instead, he could only grunt and spit at the chastising words as he ushered Bob forward. Bourg nodded that his point had been made and turned Danavas back around to lead the expedition once more. The armored rider was only vaguely aware that Elion had swooped down to fly along his right side and Talian on his left.

"You harbor doubts regarding Krill's salvation, White Rider?" she asked.

"You act to know me well, Princess Talian." Bourg replied after a moment. "No; if only to keep any hope about the Salvation of Trina, I cannot entertain doubts about the fate of only one of her cities. Are you, perchance, familiar with one of the few mentions of the Trinity in the Sacred Text? The proper Trinity may only work as *three* members."

The winged Guardian was silent for but a moment, considering the knight's words. Such a passage as had been invoked left very little room for human interpretation. However, the White Knight clearly needed his mind set at ease.

"We *three* are the Trinity proper. **You** are our Knight of Salvation, clearly above and beyond classification as a member of a mere Trinity." Talian announced. Deep in the back of her mind, Talian knew that she still harbored resentment over the classification and hoped that her own concerns had not been evident in her speech. Still, Bourg afforded a slight chuckle.

"You speak truths, Princess." Bourg announced. "Though, hardly a Fellowship containing a Celestial Guardian amongst its members is a *mere* anything. Our efforts work in concert as a full Fellowship; but only you three may be identified as the Trinity. Forward, noble Trinity. The Knight of Salvation requires an audience with Mother Superior. Perhaps I might solve the mystery of what hidden treachery has befallen this most revered and holy city."

"And it would be Mama Imperious who knows the answers?"

Helimslynch snorted, "Onward, Bob. An audience with the Mother Most Holy awaits her son."

The small mule afforded a snort of his own and carried his rider in the direction of the Bourg Mansion and the Church. No member of the company gazed into the darkness of a nearby farmhouse. Therefore, no member of the Fellowship had been the first to gaze upon an armored rider matching the Knight of Salvation. This man's armor was midnight black and the purposes governing his mission were evil ones. The Black Knight of Gorrenwrath gazed upon each member of the Fellowship for but a moment until his eyes fixed on the White Knight of Salvation. This was to be his target. The successful defeat of the Knight of Salvation could only serve to remind the man masked by the mantle of Black Knight just how powerful he truly was. A youthful lust for superiority flared in the Black Knight's mind as a midnight steed marched him forward on his own mission. He was now outside of the Fellowship's field of vision without the benefit of Talian's mystic foresight and could travel as he pleased.

As the allied members of the Fellowship reached the church, it was clear that damage had been done to the aesthetic walls of the building. Furthermore, as the parishioners who were helping to rebuild and reconstruct glared upon the Dwarven rider with some suspicion, it was evident what had been the cause of the minimal damage. The perpetrators against their house of worship had been unbelievers, perhaps in an unprovoked attack. Without an actual identity on the attacker, they were regarding a dwarf with suspicion. Finally, it was the Knight of Salvation who dismounted and addressed the worshipful believers.

"I seek an audience with Mother Superior." Bourg announced. "Fellow Trinity, aid the allies of the church in rebuilding what was broken. I must confer with Mother Superior alone."

"And shall Mother Imperious gaze upon the face of her son or her precious Knight?" Helimslynch spat, well aware of the dirty looks that he was receiving from the believers and relishing in the attention.

Bourg glared upon the Dwarven general, and disappeared into the church, his helmet firmly in place. He sought to keep Mother Superior's respect and her attention to his latest string of edicts. It would perhaps be best if she were to confer with the Knight that she had entrusted with Trina's salvation. As the armored knight entered the church, the heavy doors slammed behind him and bolted themselves for privacy. As the hero continued to the Grand Hall, he was only vaguely aware that his allies had moved as requested to help perform the necessary repairs to the exterior walls. He said a silent prayer for continued communion between the church's most loyal parishioners and the Trinity.

The interior of the Grand Hall where the worshipper's gathered appeared undamaged to the casual observer. However, the same casual observer would have easily seen the same that the Knight of Salvation did at that moment. Joto, ever vigilant, was flittering about the hall to clean up the damage in between hours of assembled worship. Indeed, as light entered into the new plate glass window and glistened against the Knight of Salvation's armor, it startled Joto into nearly dumping some stray bits of glass all over the floor again.

"I-I'm sorry but--" Joto began as he sought his composure from the startle.

"Forgive me, humble servant of the church." The Knight of Salvation's baritone timbre echoed from beneath the helmet. "I seek an audience with the Highly Exalted Lady of the Church."

Upon recognizing the intruder, Joto dumped the dustpan of glass, thereby disturbing the clean floor once more. As he turned to face the armored ally, he promptly dropped to a single knee in exaltation.

"Sh-she's not in, Knight of Salvation." Joto announced. "My apologies for the mess. This house of worship was not anticipating company this day."

"Joto, humble servant to the church and lifelong friend to the late Maxim Bourg," the Knight chuckled, "you have been my guardian and trusted teacher since crib time. You are certainly afforded the privilege to address me by name."

Joto seemed to consider whether or not such an invitation were some sort of test; then his skeletal face separated into a solid grin.

"Welcome home, Son of Bourg." He greeted him, stumbling to rise back to his feet. "What has prompted your return in the middle of your quest?"

The Knight of Salvation paused momentarily. He then raised the face shield of his helmet just enough to reveal the sincere concern and pain lining his lips.

"There are whispers that Krill would be subject to downfall by one of Gorrenwrath's agents." Jovan announced. "Each of Gorrenwrath's agents represents a cardinal sin. Do you know anything of what Krill struggles with the most?"

Joto scratched the soul patch along his rectangular chin momentarily before responding. If anyone, he surely trusted Jovan Bourg to not repeat what he said next to Mother Superior.

"For the condition that Krill is in," Joto observed, warily, "there could be any number of principal struggles. I do, however, know of someone who could be more helpful. She is in the study presently."

"Fetch my mother, friend Joto." Bourg insisted, his humble baritone echoing once more through his helmet.

Joto nodded and disappeared dutifully into the study where reconciliation was practiced between parishioners and the church elders. It wasn't a moment later that Mother Superior emerged once more. She gazed upon a single armored form kneeling before one of her pews.

"Good afternoon." Mother Superior greeted the visitor with forced gentility. "I do apologize but we do not find ourselves prepared to counsel our people in the Word this day."

"Quite alright, Mother...Superior." The unmistakable humble baritone echoed through the air and into the church elder's mind as the sun glistened and glowed off of the armor of the Knight of Salvation. "Perhaps you are prepared to receive the sage counsel that I have come to deliver instead?"

Mother Superior recognized the visitor immediately. Contrary to previous speculation, she was no happier to feast her eyes on the Knight of Salvation than she would have the Son of the Cloth.

"You come here under the guise of the one who has come to save the church." Martilla Bourg observed. "Yet speak with the tongue of the most vocal offender of our holiest practices."

"By divine interpretation of our Sacred Text, I was christened with the duty to defend all of Trina from an evil greater than any believer or disbeliever." The White Knight of Salvation insisted. "However, I do seek your pardon over any misunderstanding. I am not here to challenge the church's practices this day. What ever Evil surrounds fair Trina has given way to disastrous temptation in her most holy city of Krill. Would you have any understanding of this?"

"My parishioners have confessed nothing." Mother Superior announced. "You can observe from the damage done to this beauteous house of worship that the true evil does not exist within these walls. We are honored and blessed people here, called to glorify our message even as far as the unenlightened ear."

"I have seen the damage here, Mother Superior." Bourg observed.

"Yet, you have brought your troubles here and questioned the victims of these most recent offenses?" Mother Superior demanded.

"Ages old offenses, from one side or the other, started this." Bourg reminded her. "The Trinity is outside helping to rebuild what was defaced. They will surely stay off any heathenish assailers so long as they are here."

"We should all feel so relieved that the Trinity understands who is truly the victim in Krill." Mother Superior opined. "I have told you that I know nothing of what has caused Krill's downfall."

"I will present my qualms to Darath and the unbelievers." The Knight of Salvation replied, presenting his crucifix before Mother Superior. "A token of humblest apology; may this holy place remain protected. I petition that its veil may ring true from Western Seraphic to the Easternmost Iron Mountains; as far North as Nardot and as Southerly as neighboring Nauros and Callistra."

A sour look threatened to crease Mother Superior's lips as she accepted the generous gift of veiled protection. Nardot was where the vilest of sinners were cast and the Iron Mountains housed the Dwarf Lords, unrepentant disbelievers! However, the gracious gift of further protection presented Mother Superior with a responsibility and she took the crucifix gingerly. Just as the crucifix changed hands, the replaced plate glass window was smashed through!

Within moments, the White Knight of Salvation sprang into action and knocked Mother Superior aside to avoid the oncoming plate glass from the replaced ceremonial window. A small, round projectile of black that had damaged the Grand Hall once more clanged against armor and dropped to the floor.

"Vile heathens!" Mother Superior spat from her place of protection. "Is this the protection that the Fellowship offers me? I would not doubt that the Dwarven rider did this!"

The White Knight of Salvation approached the small projectile and turned it over in his hands.

"Rest assured that Helimslynch would never harm the church proper and does not carry a mace." The Knight of Salvation announced.

The next sound was a commotion from the outside of the church halls.

"You can't just--." The voice of one of the oldest parishioners objected.

The gut wrenching sound of steel against flesh silenced the protest with one final startled yelp to mark his last words.

As the Knight of Salvation prepped the Icarus to determine what violence had found the church, he heard the sound of the church doors buckling in from forced entry. After that, the Grand Hall was broken into in much the same fashion. WarCleaver now glistened with damaged wood chips and was slung across its Dwarven master's shoulder.

"A rider in black armor sits outside." Helimslynch announced as Armin filed into the Grand Hall next. "I think he wants a word with you, Son of Bourg. You address his grievances; we'll protect the Church Mother 'til determined otherwise."

"My blades will aid you in combat should the Icarus be lost." Armin offered.

The thought of the loss of the Icarus gave the Knight of Salvation pause. The Icarus was indeed a powerful blade; its legends of lore said so. As a blade, it had helped Maxim Bourg in combat. Outside of combat, it rested on the church walls to gather the sun's rays as a glistening cross. The thought of such a tool being damaged would have seemed preposterous. Surely, Armin knew the legends surrounding the sword and had still raised the suggestion.

"No; I must turn away a vile threat to the church and to my own home alone." Bourg observed. "I hope that you understand, Brother Elf. I need both of you to guard Mother Superior with your lives. No other invading forces may enter the building. Talian must lead the other parishioners to a place of security."

"The black rider is not here for parishioners." Helimslynch insisted. "He's here for you!"

"The parishioners are well on their way to safety and we have spotted no other rebelling unbelievers." Armin added. "Take loyal Danavas and meet your challenger!"

The Knight of Salvation afforded a nod of gratitude and exited the church as swiftly as his legs could carry him. The light of the midmorning sun glistened off of his armor as he went. The Holy Rider had to protect the church from further harm, to protect its Mother Superior, and to prevent the church loyalists from intervening where they stood no chance. There remained one choice. The Knight's crucial job was to lure the villainous rider away from the house of worship to do battle elsewhere. But first, of course, he needed to find the enemy who had come to confront him.

The echo of rushing iron footsteps alerted the Knight of Salvation in the direction that he needed to face. Within moments, a black armored arm knocked the White Knight out of the saddle and to the ground in a single strike. Danavas reared up and unleashed a startled whine at the sudden arrival of the dark armored warrior. The noble steed's protestations were silenced by the precise stab of a large black sword that the enemy knight hadn't been holding seconds before. The armor, though black, matched the Knight of Salvation's armor in texture and design. The blade, though dark, was a perfect match for the Icarus. Furthermore, the dark armored rider had successfully concealed his armor in shadow on a sunny day. Now, that he had sprung into battle, his movements were a perfect match for The Knight of Salvation. Jovan Bourg had met the enemy; and the enemy was his mirror equal. The Black Knight watched in dark satisfaction as the loud steed collapsed never to rise again. Then the armored rider returned his attention to his true victim.

"Rise and meet your superior, Illegitimate Son of the Cloth!" a deep baritone twisted in dark malice bellowed as the Black Knight arced his blade for another pass against his fallen opponent.

The assailant had referred to the Knight of Salvation as the *illegitimate* Son of the Cloth; born of a church elder and the leading voice of the unbelievers. Few children were born of such a marriage. Only *one* had ever risen to be identified as the Son of the Cloth. The dark rider knew the Knight of Salvation's identity. Worse yet, the White Knight swore to himself that he recognized his assailant's voice from somewhere.

"I said get up, Bourg!" the Black Knight bellowed. "I take no satisfaction in executing a killing stroke against such a pathetic worm who will not stand in combat. It would make me so much *prouder* to dispose of a willing opponent."

The words cut deeper than any gash that the blade could leave in the Knight of Salvation's armor. A degree of pride rested in victory. Furthermore, even the suggestion of casting a blow against a fallen man could have only come from one person who would know Bourg's identity...

"Demetrius Slade?" Bourg could barely whisper the name, rising to a single knee that he might stand up once more. Still, a boot to the chest forced him to his back once more. That same boot drove sharply into his throat where he now rested.

"I was always your opponent, by far your superior, and now, I will gladly become your executioner!" Demetrius bellowed. With that, he raised the sword once more and prepared to drive it into his pinned down opponent's chest while his boot continued to choke him.

Inches away from blacking out from lack of oxygen, Jovan Bourg wanted to crush his longtime opponent. This man who may have been his superior in couple of years of age but, as history had proven time and again, never in combat. The temptation grew to take his enemy's boot and throw the Black Knight on top of his own blade. To do so seemed to be the only way to settle in Demetrius's mind any question of who was the best.

As he neared blacking out, the Knight of Salvation knew that something had to be done. Settling an old grudge dispute once and for all may have satisfied Jovan Bourg but what would it do for Trina's fate? The dark blade was inches away from making contact and infinitely ending the White Knight's life. However, the skilled warrior freed one hand and managed to slap the blade out of the Black Knight's single-handed grip. With the sword gone and the Black Knight caught off guard, the White Knight managed to cast the villain's single iron boot aside. Such a motion sent the enemy clumsily down the hillside.

The Knight of Salvation collected his bearings, gathered the fallen blade, and watched the Black Knight roll head over heels down the hillside. He knew that the armor had protected him from any real harm in his descent. Still, the battle had been lured away from the church. The Knight of Salvation descended the hillside, bearing both his Icarus and the enemy's dark blade. Yet, that advantage only lasted long enough for the Black Knight to kick the White Knight of Salvation in the gut and force him to drop the dark blade long enough to gather up the weapon.

The Knight of Salvation was wounded once more and this was the true opportunity for the Black Knight of Gorrenwrath to take. The armored rider leveled his blade, the weapon seemingly supercharged by the mixture of hatred and superiority that the Black Knight carried with him. The blade swung with grim finality if only to strike down its latest victim. Instead, the dark blade met the Icarus with a resounding clash of steel. The Black Knight backed away, startled by the sudden transition but even more determined to satisfy his taste for victory. The Black Knight swung with more force than before. Again, blade echoed harmlessly against blade. The Black Knight unleashed a blood curdling cry of hatred and swung the dark blade a third and final time to end the Knight of Salvation's life on impact. A third time, the killing blade met the protective stroke of the Icarus; and this time, the dark blade shattered on impact.

With the loss of the sword, the Black Knight backed away from his opponent. Still, he did not back away quickly enough. The White Knight of Salvation raised the Icarus toward the Heavens once more as if preparing for a killing stroke of his own. Then, sunlight reflected and radiated off of the blade in a renewed blinding beacon of hope. As had happened to so many agents of evil before him, Demetrius was reduced to nothingness when faced down by the glowing blade.

"It may be the *illegitimate* Son of the Cloth who now rides as the Knight of Salvation." Bourg reflected. "What saddens me is that a man born of *two* church elders is the one who rides to do Gorrenwrath's bidding."

Demetrius spat from beneath his helmet and faced down his old nemesis as best he could.

"My powers were charged from Gorrenwrath." Demetrius snarled. "But the pleasure of ending your life was always meant to belong to *me*!"

"What Gorrenwrath has charged for greatness, he has destroyed after failure before, old friend." Bourg announced.

It was the sound of rushing feet behind the two combatants that prevented any response from Demetrius. Bourg turned his head just in time to spy Helimslynch and Armin on the hillside, bearing their weapons. The church was safe from harm and the Black Knight was defeated. There was only one reason for the riders of the Fellowship to have arrived bearing weapons.

"The Black Knight is vanquished." Bourg called up the hill.

"Now's the time to guarantee that his reign of terror is ended!" Helimslynch insisted, marching down the hillside with WarCleaver in hand.

The sound of a nightmarish whinny prompted Helimslynch to pause and even lower his axe as he craned his neck to see. Even Armin, his bow loaded and at the ready, appeared caught off guard as a nightmarish black steed exploded from behind the church and down the hillside. As the beast knocked the Dwarven General aside, its advance never quit until it had collected its rider. Dark steed and rider trotted out of harm's way just as the Fellowship's steeds returned.

"Shall we pursue the Dark Rider?" Armin asked, mounting Swift.

"Our primary responsibility right now is in continuing to repair the damage done to the church." The Knight of Salvation announced. "We shall leave it to Gorrenwrath to punish his own agents following their failure."

With a pair of nods, Helimslynch and Armin both returned to their positions of repairing the church as Talian and Elion returned to help. As the Trinity worked, the Knight of Salvation settled his vision on the fallen form of Danavas, his noble steed that had carried him so far on his journey. For all of the miles that Danavas had carried the burden of the Knight of Salvation, Jovan Bourg knew what he was to do. He shouldered the fallen animal to be carried to a final appropriate burial, not a place to rot right outside of the church grounds. The battle was won and it was clear to Jovan Bourg what temptation threatened a place as significant as Krill. Whether the speakers came from the church or the rebellious unbelievers, the voices always echoed proudly on listening ears. Still, whilst Krill still struggled with the temptation of pride, it was no longer powerful enough to attract Gorrenwrath's agents. Therefore, once Danavas was properly buried and the church rebuilt from destruction, the Fellowship could press on...

LUST

Young Bourg saw her from across the Grand Hall. As per usual during his mother's teachings, the Grand Hall was filled to the rafters with parishioners. But that day, in that hour, it might as well have been just those two youths. In his nineteen years, his mother's preaching had never fallen on any deaf ears of his. That day, she might have not said a word for all that Jovan Bourg was concerned.

Hundreds of able bodies stood, cutting off Jovan Bourg's view of the object of his attentions as parishioners made their mass rush to the exits following dismissal. Jovan Bourg would need to work quickly if only to have the time to speak with the young woman that had caught his eye long before. He simply had little time to entertain the oldest parishioners as the Son of the Cloth.

Jovan practically shoved a pair of elderly parishioners aside like stray cattle. He was determined to make it to the back of the church before the object of his undivided attention vanished into what could be confused for an illusion. Still, as Bourg arrived in the back of the sanctuary, she stood inches away from him as if rooted in place. It was as though she was meant to be waiting in the back of the sanctuary. That was the only intervention that Jovan Bourg needed to know.

"Your mother speaks a beautiful sermon to those who are willing to receive." The woman greeted him.

"She has her moments." Bourg conceded. Apparently, that Sunday had been one of those moments. He would have to make sure to listen carefully as his mother rehashed her talking points throughout the week if only to piece together the sermon.

There was a moment's silence that seemed as an eternity. The only topic of conversation that the young woman had presented to Bourg had been of the message of a sermon that he had never heard a single word of.

"Clearly you already know who I am." Bourg announced. "Forgive me if I should ask who you are."

"Celestra." The young woman cooed. Celestra; her name was Celestra. It was all that Jovan needed to know. What good was a surname, anyway?

"I've not seen you before; you are visiting?" Bourg asked.

The question was never answered, try as Celestra might have to do so. A firm hand settled itself on the girl's shoulder. The stony glare of a protective father pierced right through all of Jovan's intentions with laser beam precision. As Bourg promptly backed away and the startled Celestra was flung from the sanctuary, the look of wrath in those eyes resonated with the youthful Son of the Cloth as never before. Then, young Jovan Bourg promptly backed into Mother Superior and analyzed her look of absolute horror. All of his intentions had just been realized twice...

The alluring rain and tantalizing mist seemed to permanently surround the beautiful landscape of the island of Zantu. Zantu beckoned to voyagers of the Callistra Sea to make such an Eden the final port on their lonely journeys. The fact that Zantu was in fact the final port for many shipwreck victims on their journey through life could not be mistaken. Still the allure of the island's forbidden beauty blinded judgment in many a sailing crew.

The seemingly permanent lush rain of Zantu cascaded playfully on the island's shores as the mist seductively blanketed the island from prying eyes. It was the rain that kept Zantu's shores in bloom and the mist that tormented the curious by concealing the island's beauty from view from far off. Such a loss of vision enticed ships to draw nearer if only to gaze upon Zantu and be drawn into the natural glamour that greeted the eyes. After all, no past visitor had ever returned to report what Zantu truly hid.

The rain and mist represented an appealing draw to the outsider. However, to Zantu, they meant so much more and, as the two mixed together, they raised life from its rest. Even as rain dripped onto the island's shores and the mist swirled, three celestial shapes took form through the mist. The three appeared humanoid in stature. However, their shared celestial countenance and ethereal splendor begged otherwise. These three, clothed in white and radiating in a golden glow, appeared as messengers from Heaven. Many crewmen whom had beheld these three in confusion for celestial deities before had blindly sailed to forthcoming demise, never to be seen again. The leader of these three was the one called "Milana." Wherever accompanying Ensnara and Phade came from, they were oft referred to as her "sisters." The true origins of these three were shrouded in mystery; but their true intentions were more tempting than saintly. No, despite these three's illusion of purity, they served the very sinister force that had just awakened them from their slumber. Any semblance of "purity" was just one more weapon in their arsenal. Even as the three woke, they made no other move to prove their alertness for a moment. Only the sounds of the swirling mist and warm, inviting drizzle echoed through the air of the island. It was a few moments before these sounds were answered by a female voice; harmonious, enticing, and *seductive.*

"Let my sisters do as they wish to ensure the Trinity's demise." Milana announced. "Without the continued guidance of his precious Fellowship, the Knight of Salvation's final downfall will be credited to me."

The Callistra Sea carried the noble Fellowship over the waters on their next quest. Upon getting word of their destination of beautiful Zantu, it was all that Armin could do to contain his excitement. Helimslynch didn't even try to disguise his scoffing. From her place flying over the borrowed fishing boat and using her magic to guide the quest, Talian was doing all that she could to keep the opinions of their latest destination to herself. As for Jovan, he had heard whispers of many wrecked ships and lost crew members on even an island so beautiful as Zantu and he had wanted to remain in his homeland to guarantee that it had been purified of evil besides. Still, the Knight of Salvation had no such luxury and, after a brief burial ceremony for Danavas that had nearly even produced tears from Helimslynch, he mastered the helm of the fishing boat on its way to Zantu instead. There had been many whispers of the temptation that seemed to surround Zantu and the Knight of Salvation reminded himself to take great care. He was responsible for not only his own heart and mind but for those of the Trinity as well. To even think of an aura of temptation again prompted the Knight of Salvation to raise his eyes skyward to Talian. His gaze settled almost habitually on the Ring of Renecar adorning her finger. Some tale of evil echoed through that ring's origins and Bourg knew it. Still, he could not put his finger on it; he had read of the legendary ring long before and the Sacred Text would surely make no mention of an item of sorcery.

It was Elion's screech that snapped Bourg back to the reality placed in front of him. It was the fact that the mist that tantalizingly concealed the island hideaway now flowed around the ship that explained the great horned falcon's cries.

"We are nearing Zantu's shores." The Knight of Salvation announced.

"Perhaps fair Talian would use her magic to dissolve away some of this mist that we might be graced with the island's splendor." Armin called into the air, narrowing his sharp Elven eyes to concentrate enough to get the first glimpse of the island either way.

"Bah; you'll see your isle of Paradise when we all do in mere moments!" Helimslynch announced, rising up from his sleeping form and collecting WarCleaver. "Is that too long a wait, Brother Elf?"

"Hold, allies." Bourg called over his shoulder, lifting the Icarus from its hilt and aiming its blade skyward. "Talian, a burst of light that our friends' eyes might feast on the sight that lies before us."

Talian nodded consent and began aiming with the hand free of the Ring of Renecar. However, as her free hand was aimed, the ring resonated with enough energy so as to hinder the wing maiden's flight until she should utilize its power instead. Still, after a harsh struggle, Talian won the fight and aimed her free hand with a burst of light energy. The light energy found the Icarus like a homing beacon and, again, what looked like a weapon of war became a cross of peace (albeit upside down). However, that day, the light of the Icarus served another purpose and revealed sooner what would otherwise still be hidden. As Talian struggled in her new found pain and eventually landed aboard the ship once more, she joined her allies in admiring the surroundings placed before them. Helimslynch, his eyes just capable of peering over the side of the vessel, seemed impressed enough with the prospects of their journey.

"So this day, I agree with my Elven Brother." Helimslynch announced, "Zantu Proper is indeed a sight to behold!"

"Such surface level beauty may just disguise a grim interior, loyal blacksmith." Jovan observed; though his post-hypnotized tone took a little something away from the stress of his warning. "Take up your arms once more. We are preparing to dock alongside Zantu and there is no telling what its mist truly conceals. Talian, you are well enough to travel once more?"

The Celestial Guardian rose back to her feet and flapped her magnificent wings a couple of times to be certain before they carried her airborne once more.

"I...can certainly try." She announced.

Even Helimslynch appeared unconvinced of Talian's wellbeing as he dismounted the fishing ship right behind the Knight of Salvation. However, it was Armin who stayed behind long enough to assist Talian off of the ship on her own two feet until the point when even simple gliding was restored to her.

"Loose the ring." Armin advised, "I feel that it may alleviate your ailments, beautiful one."

"I said that I will travel!" Talian shouted with renewed determination. Without warning, a wave of energy flew from Talian's hands. It was all that Armin could do to dive for cover in time as Elion struggled to fly above the burst. The wave of destruction did, however, strike the ship. Only in the midst of the destruction did Talian shake her senses back together in time to realize what had just happened.

"I—I am sorry." She murmured, attempting once more to remove the ring. However, it would appear to the casual observer that she was merely toying with the band. The Ring of Renecar would not budge from her finger. Only Armin knew in the back of his mind what just had to be the truth of the winged one's struggles.

"It is alright." Armin reassured her, taking her hands comfortingly. "We are now trapped on our latest voyage; we will make the most of it. Our surroundings are quite beautiful, no?"

"Quite." Talian conceded, accepting the company of the archer considering that their other allies had such a head start already. It wasn't moments after the last two members of the expedition set forward that the veils of deception lifted just a little bit more. The mist swirled silently and lifted just enough to reveal two of the three "Sisters" of temptation.

"The Elf would already appear quite enamored with the winged one without the provocation of any of our designs, Sister Ensnara." One of the girls sneered.

"Divide those two just long enough for my mystic traps to affect the princess, Phade." Ensnara reassured her, "Then, surely your disguise magic can do the rest in alluring the Elf. The Trinity is to fall by our hands. Milana will handle the Knight of Salvation personally."

"If it is another woman who captures the attention of one the visitors to our island," Phade chuckled, "we shall be the ones responsible for his descent into lust!"

Ensnara nodded with wicked determination and stepped back under the cover of the eternal mist of beauty that she might prepare one of her dangerous mystic traps. Phade, in the meantime, concentrated for but a moment and seemed to vanish into the mist of her own accord. Camouflaged once more, she silently tracked the allies as she developed a plan to separate the Elf and Guardian just long enough for the trap to be set. Zantu, in all of its elegant glamour, would mark the Fellowship's final stand. Ensnara and Phade would see to the downfall of the allies forming the Trinity. The demise of the Knight of Salvation, or at the very least, the attempt, was in Milana's hands unless she should prove less than up to the task. When and if she failed to deliver the Knight of Salvation to the failure of temptation, even a failed effort could only weaken his spirit; especially with no Fellowship to keep him on the proper course. If Milana should disappoint Gorrenwrath, Phade would be only too happy to make the attempt of her own. If Phade failed, then Ensnara would only welcome the opportunity...

The White Knight of Salvation didn't much like the idea of splitting up the Fellowship. The act of doing so would only invite trouble on the fabled island that, for all of its surface beauty, had marked the demise of many sailing crews. Nevertheless, the Fellowship had a task to do and Bourg and Helimslynch had had a head start in heading off of the ship when Armin had taken the time to tend to Talian. The thought of Armin and Talian working as a unit, unmonitored and on an island prone to the lures of the temptation of Lust, presented another concern for the Knight of Salvation. However, the same concern could have always been there had he been working with Talian instead and he couldn't see leaving the Guardian behind at the ship. If only to take his mind from its burdens, the Knight of Salvation slowed just enough to allow Helimslynch to catch up a few extra steps once more.

"We'd allow the Elf and the Enchantress to traverse such a place of beauty alone?" Helimslynch grunted.

"To divide our forces now allows us the best chance of tracing Gorrenwrath to his true source." Bourg explained. "Take faith in the archer, General. This would present a great opportunity for him to contend with his own temptations."

For a moment, Helimslynch remained silent. When he spoke once more, his voice had lost its natural edge of scoffing cynicism and bitterness.

"You truly do believe in the presence of this unseen Evil; and he still has a name?" Helimslynch asked.

"We have not convinced you yet?" Bourg chuckled. "You do continue to selflessly aid me in my quest."

"I believe that you believe." Helimslynch announced. "I will believe in any ulterior manipulator of the hearts of men toward the hatred of war when I meet him and he has a face. To know of your leadership, Armin's faithfulness, and Talian's wisdom, however, could yet make me a believer in your Grandiose King."

Bourg chuckled to himself at the observation. He then reached to his belt sack to remove the battered and bloody copy of the Sacred Text that Danavas had been carrying. He then proceeded to hand the book to Helimslynch for their journey...

Talian knew to what heights Armin viewed her and recognized his struggles in containing his emotions. The Elven archer was doing much to leave well enough alone in his care for the Celestial Guardian, particularly in a land noted for its strong temptations toward illegitimate desire. The winged Princess could surely avoid acting on her own desires toward the archer and make his task easier. After all, for either of the two travelers to act on their desires could only raise concerns of temptation for both of them. Furthermore, the longer that Talian was around the archer who truly cared for her, the more difficult her own cares were to ignore. Something needed to be done to avoid temptation. As one path banked into two, the Celestial Guardian knew what had to be done.

"One of these paths must rejoin us with the Fellowship." Talian observed. "I feel that I am well enough that we each might take one path that one of us might reunite with our allies and signal the other. Have you any flares in your quiver, Great Hunter?"

"Indeed several, m' lady." Armin replied. "My agility, speed, and tracking abilities will carry me true along the right fork as your wings guide you along the left path. When one of us discovers the Fellowship once more, the other will be alerted by my arrows or your magic, respectively. Do take great care in your travels and if I cannot personally see to your safety, do at least take Elion."

Elion, having heard his name, raised his head from his mistress's shoulder and took to the air once more, ever on the alert. Even in the midst of danger and with the knowledge that the group had been divided, this was enough to raise a chuckle from Talian and Armin.

"Elion will not allow my downfall." Talian reassured the archer."Come, my faithful falcon. We will let the archer go his own way to freedom."

Within moments, Talian spread her majestic wings once more and joined her ally in the air, leaving only Armin to watch them go. For the briefest moment, the archer remained rooted in his place between the two paths. Talian had tried her best to reassure him that she would be safe under the protection of her oldest ally and Armin knew that Elion could protect her better than he might have. Still, he did not like the idea of splitting up the forces yet again. As beautiful as the island was, it remained unfamiliar territory.

Finally, Armin determined that traversing separate paths was the better of two ideas if only to avoid any undue distractions of temptation and to find Gorrenwrath that much faster. Besides, Talian was far ahead by now and Armin was losing time in tracking down the Evil at its direct source or at least finding his allies again. The archer had barely begun down his own path after arming himself with his blades in anticipation of danger. With the path clear once more, the tantalizing mist swirled away just enough to reveal Phade once more.

"I thought that that love struck fool would never leave!" Phade mused, both aloud and over the telepathic link that she shared with her "sisters."

"But a love struck fool is our favorite kind." Ensnara's telepath echoed through her mind.

"Yes; of course, dear sister." Phade conceded impatiently. "The winged one has left down the left fork. Once your mystical trap devices have successfully felled her, it will be all of the easier to manipulate the Elf into casting the Dwarf to defeat for us."

Within moments, the mist surrounding Zantu intensified once more to conceal Phade's presence as she moved back down the path to see for certain that Talian was captured. Certainly, Ensnara could be counted on to trap ordinary voyagers. Still, the Fellowship was not represented by ordinary voyagers. Besides, if Phade was going to perform her task correctly, she would need to see Talian's face once she was captured. On the off-chance that Ensnara should fail to truly trap Talian, Phade would always be there to finish the task for her master, Gorrenwrath.

Talian and Elion continued down their selected path by blind faith. Elion let out a screech as the pair continued. There had been a time when Talian's magic had allowed her to decipher what her feathered waif was communicating to her. Still, lately, try as she might to read the falcon's thoughts, her magic had deprived her of the opportunity as the mystic ring on her finger pulsated instead. Somewhere in the back of her mind, Talian's mystic foresight was clamoring for her attention as well, constantly warning her of danger. Still, its warnings were indeterminate as the Ring of Renecar only pulsated with each attempt at mystic vision. The loss of so much power was enough to weigh Talian down. Furthermore, the payoff of increased magic was starting to be less and less appealing. The winged princess barely managed to land, her wings weighed down. She again took a moment out of her journey to attempt to remove the Ring of Renecar from her finger and its power from her life. Still, the ring held fast as if of its own accord with each attempt to remove the enchanted device.

"I confess that I do not like this, my feathered friend." Talian observed, trying once again at removing the ring. Elion, recognizing his mistress's dilemma, flew into the air and his golden horns glistened with mystic energy of their own. Still, even the combined efforts were to no avail. Within moments, however, Elion did not so much give up on the task as suddenly stop, glaring over his mistress's shoulder.

As Elion's power built up once more and he unleashed a warning shriek, Talian turned that she might face the same direction as her falcon. Still, it was too late. Within moments, an Iron Vine lashed out as would a lariat and ensnared the hand that contained the Ring of Renecar. Talian's free hand instantly surged with mystic energy and aimed at the ensnaring Iron Vine. Still, a second serpentine vine seized her free hand as well and the destructive burst of magic flew in the wrong direction. Even with her arms pinned, however, Talian knew that she had every opportunity to escape the trap.

By really concentrating, Talian managed to flap her once magnificent wings once more and pull against the Iron Vines that her people could naturally control in the realms of Seraphic Forest. Still, it took all of Talian's focus to attempt to escape instead and her powers of control had been greatly reduced since adorning the Ring of Renecar. As two more Vines shot out of nowhere and seized the enchantress by both legs, she reached the conclusion that only the most destructive potentials of her powers had been increased by the Ring. The fact remained that she, as with all of the Guardians, had not been given her powers to destroy.

It took one final ditch effort to yank the Iron Vines near their break-ing point. Still, the effort was for naught and the natural entanglements pulled back that much harder, sending the ethereal Guardian crashing helplessly into the forest. Elion saw his mistress's plight and his golden horns glistened with magic once more. Still, a burst of purple pollen mixed with the natural mist of below and Elion dropped to the ground in a deep slumber, his protests and his magic silenced.

The purple pollen, common in the tantalizingly sweet Ambrosia Flower, threatened Talian with its bittersweet aftereffects of eternal rest as she was drawn by the mystic Iron Vines into Zantu's fabled Forest of Desire. As the vines slammed Talian into a giant tree, injuring her wings, she struggled from the bittersweet pollen of the Ambrosia. Instantly, a golden mist swelled and swirled around the ethereal Guardian as well. As she struggled against the Iron Vines, the sleeping spell of the Ambrosia, and the golden mist, two new forms took shape in front of the captive.

"Most impressive, dear sister." Phade cackled, "You have planned well for our guest's arrival."

"The enticing pollen of sweet Ambrosia prevents her escape and keeps her bird from following. The golden mist of the Phylos Tree saps even her magic. The Iron Vines keep her secured." Ensnara chortled, "We know the good Princess well. Milana was born an ethereal Guardian until her powers were taken away in punishment and she was banished to this prison of eternal beauty."

"I remember well." Phade replied, "It was in Milana's blind vengeance that we two were created of her remaining powers. Now, lest you think that your job is done..."

"I've not forgotten." Ensnara interjected, casting a sweep of her hand in the direction of the Phylos Tree that had served as the catalyst for her trap. Responding to the mystic signal, another Iron Vine loosed itself from a nearby branch and struck the barely struggling Talian in the wings. The throbbing blow loosed a single feather and Phade collected the prize.

It was all that Talian could do to stay awake, much less be aware of what was happening around her. She was trapped on Zantu and these women, though she could not hear them, were clearly her captors. Still, while the Celestial Guardian knew her own fate, she could not determine what was to become of the rest of the Fellowship; of Armin. It was that final sad thought that silenced Talian's mind just before her eyes settled once more on the Ring of Renecar. That accursed ring had driven her to madness and to use her powers at their most destructive. Furthermore, if this pollen were not taking her powers from her, then the mystic council would surely do the deed before casting her out, Princess or no.

"Great Almighty," Talian managed as she struggled against blacking out, "Think not that I am praying for myself. I have failed bitterly and misused magic that has come generously from You. My time is nearing its end and I shall be presented before judgment in my passing. Take this Ring. Rob it of its cruel power where I have failed to do so. Continue to guide the Fellowship in their paths. Make them much stronger and more vigilant than I that they might not repeat these errors of mine. Take great care to watch over the noblest among Elves, Great Almighty. I do lo--"

A harsh cackle, this one clearly audible to Talian's ears, silenced her personal petition. Her captors now stood inches away from her ensnarement but out of range of the Ambrosia or Phylos pollen.

"Poor, poor dear Princess among Guardians!" one of the women mused, turning the dislodged feather around in her finger tips and holding the displaced member tantalizing inches away from the struggling victim. Before Talian's very eyes, that single feather in the enemy's hand sprouted into wings of magnificence across the other woman's back. As the wings sprouted, even her garments of white turned to green iron.

"Oh, please; do not let us two so rudely interrupt your prayer time!" the shape-shifting woman continued in a voice that was sounding less like her own but more like one that was quite familiar to Talian. "After all, what good would your face be to our cause without your most harmonious voice?"

Ensnara had a hard time deciding which was more entertaining; Phade's cruel jibes or Talian's pathetic attempts at struggling to stay awake. Then, Phade attempted to complete the spell of disguise on her face, shrieked at the response, and it was decided what was clearly most amusing.

"My face!" Phade shouted, "It is hideous! How is this?"

"Her beauty...it is..." Ensnara barely managed through fits of merciless laughter, "...ethereal by nature. Her pure innocence...makes her... unblemished."

"Silence that absurd cackling and fetch me the helmet and tiara!" Phade demanded before switching back to Talian's voice even as she restored her own face to normalcy rather than its haggard transformation. "With the mask to hide my face, her voice will serve its purpose nicely to allure the archer to prompt the Dwarf's demise. That will secure his own downfall into sin."

Ensnara grumbled against her sister but, with a sweep of her hand, commanded two more Iron Vines to seize and deliver the helmet and the tiara lest she step into range of her own trap. Only as Phade secured the tiara and masked helmet to her head did she clearly see the Ring of Renecar glistening on the Guardian's finger as if beckoning to the common observer.

"The Ring of Renecar, my master's ring, on the finger of a simple wielder of *healing* magic!" Phade spat, forgetting momentarily of the trap as she approached the Ring. "Surely, such a ring deserves to adorn the finger of one of our master's allies before it is used for his destruction!"

"The destruction has already been done to Talian. She will see punishment for all that her powers have done." Ensnara announced, settling a guiding hand on Phade's shoulder. "Go do your task of casting the remainder of the Trinity to failure; I have done my portion."

At the mere suggestion that Phade leave the ring ignored, the sorceress of disguise magic launched a destructive burst at Ensnara to force her off of her and into her own trap. With that, the cruel sorceress lunged for the Ring of Renecar, oblivious to the mystic pollen that would take her magic powers. As she went to loose the ring from Talian's finger, however, a mystic barrier tossed her backwards and into a nearby tree, her magic still working at full potential but the helmet and tiara knocked slightly askew from the crash. As Phade rose from the ground once more, she readjusted the mask and tiara and set out on her way. The Ring of Renecar and certainly the plight of the other two sorceresses were forgotten once more. The remaining enchantress still had a job to do to guarantee that Milana could impact the Knight of Salvation without outside interference...

Armin followed his path to a grassy knoll; the perfect loft to observe out the furthest distance. Within moments, the Elven hunter had mounted the grassy mound, praying that Talian had already found the others and had simply neglected to warn him. The departure had been too long ago. If his Elven eyes did not see Talian alongside the rest of the Fellowship... he couldn't bear to finish the thought. Armin crouched on his new perch and narrowed his superior Elven eyes to concentrate just ahead and block out surrounding distractions. In the great distance, Armin could see Helimslynch and the Knight of Salvation but did not see Talian or Elion right away. Deciding that they could possibly be a distance off yet, Armin remembered their deal, replaced his swords in his belt, and raised his bow instead. He then knelt to collect a flare arrow from his satchel...

The flare arrow would have never been necessary. A beauteous winged woman landed on the grassy knoll right behind the archer as an arrival right out of a beautiful dream. Still, Armin knew better. He promptly dropped the arrow to his feet in relief before dropping to a profound kneel before such ethereal beauty as Talian presented before him.

"You had missed me?" Talian's voice echoed on Armin's Elven ears like a sweet ocean breeze.

"I can perhaps cancel the search now." Armin quipped, any semblance of a joke in his voice replaced with relief. "It seems that you are still well enough to travel and the others are only several hundred yards ahead. Wait; what of Elion?"

"Elion is investigating something that he thought he saw in the great distance." Talian announced. "He will catch up briefly."

The fact that Elion had just been dismissed so casually was enough to give Armin pause for the briefest moment. Still, he collected his footing and his bow once more. However, as he moved to catch up to the others, he was paused once more by the fact that Talian had made no commitment to following. Her wings stayed folded stubbornly.

"You can clearly see from here that our 'Fellowship' does not miss us so much." Talian sneered.

Armin turned to face the group's receding backs once more as he loaded a flare arrow to alert the others to wait.

"They determined that it was important to investigate our new sur-roundings before moving on." Armin announced. "It was whispered that even beautiful Zantu is succumb to vile temptation."

"And to investigate these shores was more important than to assist me when it was needed most?" Talian demanded.

"They had determined that I would assuredly aid you as needed." Armin insisted. However, he did unstring the flare arrow, resituate it in his arsenal, and shoulder his bow before turning to face the Guardian.

Beneath the mask of the Celestial Guardian, Phade smiled wickedly. She was starting, slowly but surely, to get through Armin's carefully crafted defenses of loyalty. It would take but one final stroke to break down the final barriers altogether.

"Talian," Armin spoke to her, settling a hand on either shoulder, "what has become of you of late? Ever since you had received that ring--Talian, where is the Ring of Renecar?"

"My powers had become too great for even Renecar's Ring to contain. It is destroyed." Talian announced, seeming to gaze off in the distance beneath her masked helmet. "Clearly, the Knight of Salvation will work just fine with the Dwarven General alone."

"Let us make haste to catch up, fairest Talian." Armin replied again, removing his hands from her shoulders and turning once more to face the retreating group.

"There is no hurry to reconnect with them when we can continue to be alone on this island Paradise." Talian insisted, placing a comforting hand of her own seductively on Armin's shoulder. "Surely such a brave, strong, handsome general as Helimslynch can defend noble Jovan from danger just fine. However, now would perhaps be the best opportunity to alert to them that their true allies have returned."

Armin promptly pulled forcefully away from the seductive hand on his shoulder. His muscles tensed with anticipation. His teeth were adjoined in a gnash of envy. His eyes radiated a spiteful fire. His vision was focused on the "brave, strong, handsome" Helimslynch, the unbeliever. What happened next took only moments as an arrow (not Armin's flare) caressed the bowstring, and Armin fired the projectile (not harmlessly at the air)...

As the pair trudged along the shoreline of Zantu, Helimslynch was concerned as to what had become of the others. Truly, as far as Elves went, Armin was an ally whom had earned the respect of the general. As to Talian, while the Dwarf adamantly dismissed the explanation of her origins or her powers, he could not deny that her powers were necessary relief for their quest. As Helimslynch turned to insist once more that the Knight of Salvation at least allow him to turn back and look for the others, a low flying projectile pierced through the general's chest. It was the last thing that he would ever feel.

Jovan Bourg, walking right beside his Dwarven ally, had seen the projectile and certainly seen his ally fall. Within moments, the Knight of Salvation sprang into action and accepted the form of the mortally wounded Dwarf before removing the projectile from the injury. He had already determined where the arrow must have come from to have struck down the Dwarf from behind. Upon closest examination, he certainly recognized the arrow...

Armin's Elven ears had practically heard the gut-wrenching impact of the arrow from his perch several hundred yards away. They had certainly heard the cry of pain and his eyes had seen what had happened. Furthermore, there was no question in the archer's mind what had happened as he numbly dropped his bow to his side and whirled to face his female ally.

"The mighty hunter has again struck down the savage beast." Talian observed in her melodious chuckle.

"The Ring has truly poisoned your heart before it was destroyed!" Armin cried, "You have pushed me to shooting down our own ally!"

"It was a rather delicate push, noble archer." Talian declared. All at once, Armin's eyes went wide and his body tensed, his hand resting on a blade. Talian's voice no longer sounded like its own; and those were certainly no words of hers. Without warning, a single blade lunged out and smashed the mask open to reveal the startled face beneath it.

"What bewitchery is this?" Armin demanded. "What has become of the true Talian, foul sorceress of deceit?"

Phade could only cackle wickedly at the archer's attempt to threaten her. The wings that completed her disguise exploded out of their sedentary state and knocked the Elf backward with ease before allowing her flight to escape. Within moments, Phade was gone from the scene and Armin was picking himself up clumsily off of the ground and gathering up his weapons. At this time, Bourg arrived at the mound. He carried their now lifeless ally under one arm and the offending arrow in the other hand.

"Armin!" Bourg boomed, the humble baritone long gone from his voice. "What had possessed you to shoot our own ally, my friend?"

Armin lowered his weapons back to their stationary positions and bowed his head in remembrance.

"I-I was bewitched, noble Knight." Armin confessed. "A wicked enchantress substituted for Talian. It was she who manipulated my...envy, Son of Bourg. Envy that we had been left behind at the ship. Envy that she had spoken so kindly of noble Helimslynch..."

"She did not string the arrow and pull the bowstring; those actions were yours." Bourg interjected. "If what you claim as truth is so, then the Trinity gathered to help me on my own path has already fallen. Talian is lost, Helimslynch is dead, and you have fallen the furthest of everyone. Find a boat and return to Krill. The church will gladly take you in as one of its own."

"A-and what of you, honorable Knight?" Armin asked, badly shaken not so much because he was being sent home but because he deserved no better.

All was silent for a moment as the Knight of Salvation considered the answer and reached for a crucifix that was no longer affixed to his neck.

"The Sacred Trinity has shared my burdens for this long on our voyage." Bourg announced. "Perhaps it was long enough that I might succeed in what remains. Here; take my copy of the Sacred Text that you may lean to and acquire its wisdom during your journey home."

"Then I shall take the Sacred Text for the journey home and the body of my fallen Dwarven brother to be properly buried on Iron Mountain." Armin vowed before dropping to a proper kneel. "Godspeed, Son of Church and White Knight of Salvation."

"Rise, respected Elven Archer and noble friend of the Cloth. Take our fallen ally and the Sacred Text gifted to you." Bourg decreed, surrendering the Text to his ally, "Safe journeys."

Jovan laid Helimslynch's body alongside the dislodged weapons as Armin staggered back to his feet in all of his personal weakness. The archer struggled with more to say on the issue at hand. Still, the White Knight of Salvation turned on his heels and vanished into the mist without another word on the subject. Armin was left alone to return to Krill's shores after turning the departed Dwarven general over to the ceremonial kilns of Iron Mountain with his deepest regrets. However, Armin could not obey the directive to charter another ship back home yet.

"You shall rest in peace on this island Paradise a while longer, strong Dwarf." Armin observed, gathering up his weapons. "I must satisfy myself that Talian is safe; or that I have exhausted all of my resources to search."

Without another word, Armin vanished into the mist surrounding Zantu. For the briefest moment, that entrancing mist became an impenetrable fog. As that fog lifted, Armin and the body of Helimslynch were gone, leaving the Elf's weapons and Sacred Text in its wake...

He was alone on his taxing quest for the very first time. Even if Jovan Bourg couldn't help but wonder if he could possibly succeed over extreme Evil and temptation, the White Knight of Salvation needed to press forth. If nothing else, then the White Rider that the Sacred Text reported of so highly at least owed fair Trina his very best attempt.

For the briefest moment, the Knight of Salvation paused in the middle of the tropical paradise. His mission could surely wait for a few more moments as he gathered strength, diligence, and determination in his travels in the absence of the allies. Gingerly, the Knight of Salvation unsheathed the Icarus and spun the weapon blade down with practiced motions. He then determinedly but cautiously anchored the "weapon" into the ground.

As the Icarus attracted the sun's rays even through the mist, the Knight of Salvation dropped to a humble kneel before the glistening cross in the middle of the island. The members of the Fellowship needed protection. Helimslynch was owed a great debt of gratitude and an early inheritance into the Ethereal Kingdom. Peace and prosperity between the believers and unbelievers was still a goal to strive toward. Furthermore, the Holy Fellowship had pushed Bourg this far into his journey and the Knight of Salvation would require additional strength and determination to finish the task.

"Excuse me." A female voice threatened to cut into Jovan's thoughts.

"My sincerest apologies. If you would be so kind as to give me one moment." Bourg interjected from his place of genuflection before the Icarus's radiance.

"Of course, noble one." The visitor purred as a single hand was placed to Bourg's armored left shoulder. "It is not every day that our island draws a visitor so diligent, and striking as well."

Something in the woman's intonations cut through the last of Bourg's carefully crafted defenses. His time of genuflection disturbed, he was drawn to get a good look at the speaker behind him. The Knight of Salvation staggered back to his feet beneath the weight of armor and turned to face the local whom had intruded on his personal reflection. Upon facing the woman, the Knight of Salvation was only drawn to remove the helmet. The face of Jovan Bourg needed to gaze upon this beautiful woman with ease. Indeed, such a woman reflected what Celestra had meant to a slightly younger Son of the Cloth without the innocence reflected in Armin's feelings for Talian. There was no denying it; the last of Bourg's defenses were gone.

"You are lost?" the woman asked, advancing on him once more.

"I have been stranded in your most glorious paradise." Bourg amended. "Should there be a port nearby, fair lady? I fear that this is urgent."

"Is something so urgent as to tear you from our shores so soon?" the woman insisted, her voice still pealing smoothly on Bourg's ears as she approached until she was inches from contact with him. "I am Milana."

"Jovan, Son of Bourg." Bourg responded. Between the harmony of this woman's voice, her closeness tempting him to feel her touch, and the distinct beauty of Zantu, Jovan's soul had given way to darkness a long time before. He could not even remember the need for the armor, nor for the Icarus Blade. The view of Trina's wellbeing from Zantu's perspective was refreshing and calming.

"You?" Milana gushed, drawing her very closest and caressing Jovan's offered cheek. "You are the Knight of Salvation?"

Such a reminder was enough to snap Bourg free of the trance of mind and heart that this beautiful woman, her island, and its alluring mist had placed over him. Jovan Bourg was more than the privileged Son of the Cloth. He remained Trina's *Knight of Salvation*. As the Knight of Salvation, he needed to recover his senses and never lose his moral conviction again.

As Milana continued in her advances, Bourg took a sidestep in retreat. The blazing radiance of the Icarus did not disappoint his intentions. The burst of golden glow was enough to blind Milana and paralyze her advances just long enough for the Knight of Salvation to resituate the helmet on his head. Here, his vision was slightly obscured once more and he was protected from the enchantress's direct caress.

As Milana instinctively shielded her eyes with one hand, her free hand shot out to desperately try to allure the Knight of Salvation once more. Still, the hand brushed armor and the beautiful woman situated before the Knight gave way to the mist surrounding the island. Elsewhere on Zantu, the other two enchantresses were absorbed into the tantalizing haze. Finally, the enchanting fog separated and rose into the sky to give way to clouds and reveal Zantu's shores for the world to feast its eyes upon at whatever distance it chose. The Knight of Salvation could only raise his blade in his bewilderment and carry on in search of a harbor and ship.

A welcoming rain caressed Zantu's shores with gentle dew as the Knight of Salvation reached the docks of Polaris Harbor to find the one vessel that remained in one piece. Bourg prayed that that one vessel would guide him to his next destination and one step closer to defeating

Gorrenwrath's menace. Before he could request guidance as to what the next leg of his quest should be, however, he heard a familiar screech and glanced up into the rain to gaze upon a great falcon with brilliant horns of gold.

"Elion." The Knight of Salvation sighed in relief. "Welcome home, faithful bird. Perhaps you know where the next evil agent of Gorrenwrath rests?"

Elion screeched once more and planted himself in the crow's nest. After seeming to consider for a moment, the falcon finally did respond to Bourg's request. Within moments, his golden horns glistened and enveloped the front of the ship in a guiding light. Such magic drew the ship out to sea and to the next object of the White Rider's quest...

GORRENWRATH

For as long as Trina existed, there rested Gorrenwrath above her shores. A black mist of Evil seeking to exact destruction over such beauty as represented by the planet, the Great Evil sought to destroy the planet through storms. Yet, no natural disaster would give way to Trina's demise. No, Trina was special; it would not fall before evil's dominance as others before her. There would have to be another way. However, Gorrenwrath was born of a time before all ages. Such an Evil could certainly afford to bide his time for a more opportune moment.

As Gorrenwrath wryly observed the world of Trina for a means of destruction, there came the arrival of the people. As humans, these were more emotional than rational and inherently suspicious of anything different from them. Furthermore, the people were already arriving in clearly defined factions of worshipful believers and cynical unbelievers. This conquest would prove all too simple of a task for Gorrenwrath. He could spare the brunt of his energies for more difficult conquests. Nevertheless, to manipulate the suspicions, prejudices, and hatred in the minds and hearts of mammon was not an opportunity for Gorrenwrath to pass up altogether. Yes, he would pluck at man's hateful nature of the Other; and watch Trina pull itself apart in war.

The plan had pressed on unabated for ages and centuries. Children of the believers looked upon children of the unbelievers as enemies without ever knowing why. Children of the unbelievers regarded children of the believers with suspicion and cynicism without question. Then, as Trina teetered on the brink of self-destruction and Gorrenwrath was beginning to turn his gaze outward toward other worlds to fall beneath his terror, there rode in a rider in white armor. He bore the Icarus of his father, he championed the righteousness of a Savior who was part of his mother's teachings, and he had banded together a loyal Trinity.

Maxim Bourg had been a man of rage against the Cloth. Martilla Bourg was a pompous old fool who could not see her personal shortcomings, nor what had resulted, through her religious prattling. Then, Jovan Bourg rode in on his armored stallion with both of the parents best attributes and very few of their shortcomings. Furthermore, for the shortcomings that the reported White Knight of Salvation did carry, the Fellowship of the Trinity had helped him overcome. This Fellowship of four sought to fell Gorrenwrath by working together in a way that his full legions, headed by seven lieutenants, could never understand.

Gorrenwrath's prime agents had failed in their missions and the Trinity had fallen to sin. Both factions knew the same price as they now hung lifelessly over a world that was doomed to loss. Just above the destruction of Mount Lyr, former Heads of State and the Church now lay lifeless and empty alongside the Great Evil's failed legions. The heroic Trinity, lost to capture, death, and sin, now hung aimlessly beside the fallen soldiers of the rebel unbelievers. Soon, all of Trina would only know of the punishment of eternal captivity. But not before the Knight of Salvation, the Son of the Cloth, paid the biggest debt of all...

Mount Lyr loomed in the great distance. Its shores kept the sands of Scilia from where the Callistra and Polaris Seas met. The Knight of Salvation was awakened from his rest by Elion's insistence to gaze upon the majestic hideaway of lore for the most important representatives of Church and State; now, their remote burial.

"Mount Lyr." Bourg reflected, grimly. "Has Daz freed himself from imprisonment?"

Elion screeched in consternation and his golden horns projected a mystic spiral of light to the sky. Before long, that mystic spiral took on the face of what waited at the mountain peak.

"Gorrenwrath." Bourg gasped the name, "Mount Lyr, once a place of such glorious majesty, shall mark my final victory over the Greatest Evil; or my final stand against it. It is disheartening how far the Mount Lyr of lore has fallen. It is not just the resting grounds for greedy Heads of State and Church but the space on which Gorrenwrath himself awaits my arrival. I thank you for guiding me here, friend Elion; but I must fight this battle alone."

As the boat moved up alongside Mount Lyr where Bourg could depart the ship but the ship would remain undamaged, Elion screeched in consternation of the latest request. Still, Bourg remained insistent as he secured himself safely to the mountainside.

"I must face this evil alone, faithful Elion. The Fellowship has already given their lives for my cause." The Knight of Salvation announced, beginning his ascent. "Guide this boat to Callistra's home port, then return to the Seraphic Forest from which you joined our expedition to rest."

Elion gazed longingly upon the Knight of Salvation's retreating form for a moment longer. Still, in the back of the falcon's mind, he knew that the White Rider had spoken with wisdom beyond even his own wishes. Elion's mystic horns glistened gold once more as his eyes took on the same supernatural hue. Within moments, the ship obediently sailed away from the side of Mount Lyr and to the far off port of Callistra.

The climb to Lyr's peak had never been an easy task. It was partially how the politicians and religious leaders had been afforded their privacy. Certainly, that ascent was not made any easier after the Knight of Salvation had spent many days fending off agents of temptation. His body aching and spirit weary, Jovan Bourg reached the peak of Mount Lyr by nightfall. In his spent condition, knowing that he was facing Evil's source, gone was Jovan's humility. It was replaced by a sense of rage that the Knight of Salvation should have never revealed.

"**GORRENWRATH!**" The Knight of Salvation howled into the Heavens at the top of his lungs. Then, as additional insult to the weakness of his revealed anger, the Knight of Salvation unsheathed the Icarus. The thought of facing Gorrenwrath made him determined that the first stroke of the mighty weapon of war would have to be its last as well.

Within moments, even the ruins of Mount Lyr gave way to the inky blackness of night fall. The Knight of Salvation stood in the dead center of an eclipse devoid of sight or sound, his weapon still at the ready.

Instantly, intense light surrounded the Knight of Salvation. It forced him to give way to blindness until he could shield his eyes from the oncoming light. It was then that The Knight of Salvation realized that he was not gazing directly upon stars. He was gazing directly into huge prisms of light, each of which contained a lifeless humanoid form. Some of the imprisoned forms surrounding Bourg looked familiar; others did not. However, all were clearly human.

Suddenly, a dark rumbling laugh from nearby called the Knight of Salvation's attention dead center into the empty space. No crystalline imprisonments were in front of him. However, a pair of glowing red eyes that seemed to pierce his soul floated there.

"You would elicit the name of Gorrenwrath as if he were a mere nuisance?" the voice of the Great Evil demanded.

"For Trina's triumph, I would do more to you than to scream your name, Gorrenwrath!" the Knight of Salvation declared. "Your evil has rested here for too long. Where are you that I might end its reign once and for all?"

"Perhaps I am right here." answered the voice from right in front of the Knight.

Without warning, a dark blade smashed into the side of the Knight of Salvation's helmet, slashing into the left side of Bourg's face and across his ear. With a declaration of pain, the Son of the Cloth whirled and reflexively raised the Icarus to deflect a second strike. What the boy came face to face with was a crystalline prison that was clearly empty. Approaching was a dark warrior that represented the Knight of Salvation's mirror equal in armor and weapon if not in intention. This was not Gorrenwrath; it was an excuse to toy with Jovan one final time.

Bourg struggled and strained against the Black Knight of Gorrenwrath within the darkened backdrop that concealed the villain so well. Finally, the Knight of Salvation raised a single boot and kicked the Black Knight away from him. Demetrius Slade recovered his footing at the last moment and lunged once more with his blade, this time toward the Knight of Salvation's armored breast plate. Still, the Knight dodged once more and threw a shoulder block at the villain. The latest attempt stunned the armored assassin and sent him reeling back toward the crystalline prison. Within moments, the prison sprang back to life and seemed to draw its captive back inside. With the Black Knight imprisoned lifelessly once again, Bourg whirled once more to face the vast empty blackness.

"I have bested your Black Knight once before without being driven to slay him and I have just repeated the triumph." The Knight of Salvation announced. "I implore you again, wretched Gorrenwrath; reveal yourself and face me personally if you are unafraid!"

Another sinister chuckle was elicited from the dark and Bourg felt a pair of eyes glaring at him from his left once more. Only as the hero turned to look did he realize that the eyes of a cobra had deceived him into thinking that he was now facing down Gorrenwrath. As the cobra lunged for the boy, a giant, dull grey demon did the same. As the vicious cobra lunged at one of the Knight of Salvation's iron boots, however, he got another idea.

The mystic creature weaved its way around a single boot, seeking the strength to crush through the iron and into his victim's leg. The Knight of Salvation, however, had been fully prepared for the assault. He thrust forward with his right leg, propelling the angry cobra airborne and around Drax's head. Before the confused cobra could crush the life out of his new victim, it was absorbed back into its crystal prison with the lifeless form of Rumios. Drax, in turn, was returned to his own sedentary state alongside the prison containing Mynos.

Without warning, a chill wind of slothfulness fell over the Knight of Salvation as several chilling chords of seduction rang through the blackness of the darkened dimension. As the haunting chords struck Bourg's exposed ear, however, he came to realize that they were deafened. With vigor, Bourg drove the Icarus against the invisible ground and forced himself to move. As the blade traversed the landscape, its painful shriek outhollered the lulling choruses of lust until they were silenced in defeat once more.

"The slaves to your evil have failed you again and the Master of Evil still will not show his face!" Bourg bellowed into the blank of space.

"The Son of the Cloth is hardly worth my personal efforts." Gorrenwrath declared. "Your father's *wrath* is clearly showing the longer you stand before me; and your mother's *pride* in every word leveled against me. However, if you wish me to show my face, I will treat it as a last request."

Several arrows fired out of the darkness to the right of the Knight of Salvation without warning. It was all that Bourg could do to roll to one side in time and raise the Icarus as a shield. He had recognized the precise accuracy of those arrows but...no, it was impossible...

In the midst of the arrows, a giant axe flew forward without warning and smashed Bourg's body armor, threatening his chest with shrapnel. Then a mystic burst flew from the darkness. Bourg swung the Icarus with all of the might that he had left to muster. Still, to deflect the blow in the direction that Gorrenwrath's voice kept coming from, was enough to not only propel him backwards but to sever the Icarus's blade as well. The blast of magic struck on seemingly harmless impact to illuminate the dimension. It revealed just enough light to reveal the three faces that Bourg had hoped he would never have to see in a place of evil.

"You are called the 'Knight of Salvation,' and you left me to be lost to our enemies!" Talian announced, her words cutting deeply into Bourg's right ear. "You left my purity of conscience at the mercy of the Ring of Renecar!"

"You abandoned me in a time when I had fallen my furthest into temptation!" Armin snarled, readying his bow once more. "I trusted you to keep my talents and loyalty as my family would not. Instead, you abandoned me in my moment of darkness!"

"I believed in your cause and you let me die!"Helimslynch bellowed.

"Has the proposed Savior, a mere *boy*, failed so many who only gathered at his side to support him in his encounters?" Gorrenwrath chuckled from nearby, now visible and floating toward the hero. "Soon his own fate will be yours and holy Trina will be ripe for destruction. You have come far to pay the greatest debt of all of those who have fallen before me, Jovan. I do owe you that. Now, do you wish to fight back against your Sacred Trinity; or forfeit your life that I might spare ONE member's?"

Bourg thought for a maybe a moment. He then whirled to face the phantom situated in front of him before remembering that he was facing Gorrenwrath unarmed.

"That would not be a promise that you are inclined to keep,

Gorrenwrath." Bourg declared. "And those shades are *not* the members of my Fellowship!"

As if on command, the three members of the Fellowship faded away into Milana, Phade, and Ensnara.

"Where are the true members of the Trinity?" Bourg demanded.

"Near enough to their own fates, I can assure you; unless a selfless sacrifice can be arranged." Gorrenwrath insisted. "It was, after all, printed in your own Sacred Text that some lives would have to be sacrificed that all may live."

The words were true. Gorrenwrath's familiarity with the Sacred Text had been undervalued. The Text's pages had warned several times that in the search for greatness and prosperity, some would have to die to save others. Bourg removed the remaining half of his damaged helmet and cast aside his broken blade. He presented himself before Gorrenwrath in the rags of a farmer's child, save for the gauntlets and leggings that still adorned his arms.

"Yes, yes; present yourself before your superior in the fullness of your inferiority, child!" Gorrenwrath clucked, the dark robes flowing back to reveal skeletal hands already glowing with dark energy.

"If I invite myself to ruin," Bourg queried, the humility restored to his voice and movements, "you will spare the Trinity?"

"One sacrifice for ONE life, foolish boy!" Gorrenwrath boomed, though the sneer clearly pointed out his lack of intention to spare *any* lives in his wake as he got a closer look at his victim. "You have removed the crucifix of protection from its place around your neck! This death shall be disappointingly simple."

As dark energy built up in Gorrenwrath's hands, he cast a sweeping gesture toward his victim. Only the sound of movement could distract the dark lord from his task at hand and he whirled around in confusion.

"If one sacrifice should spare one life," a familiar voice cut off the dark sorcerer as a new form took shape right behind him, armed with a bow and arrow, "then shouldn't we feel so lucky that for the Trinity, Jovan Bourg would gladly give his life three times?"

"Yes; and he would perish a thousand times more if it meant that Trina would be spared." Added a second voice as a second form took place in the shadows behind Gorrenwrath.

"The alleged Gorrenwrath, I presume?" a gruff bark disturbed the proceedings. "A pleasure to see you face to face. If one must die that all may live, let us arrange for your demise!"

Gorrenwrath's moment of greatness had been interrupted, however temporarily. Still, he clearly had enough power to cast aside the gnats that represented the Trinity as well. His great moment of triumph had merely been temporarily postponed.

Gorrenwrath whirled on the Trinity without warning, ready to unleash the full brunt of his powers to kill the lot of them before returning his focus to the demise of the Knight of Salvation. Still, as the Great Evil released his powers, the sting of iron against his back threw off his concentration. The dark energy meant for the Trinity was cast against Gorrenwrath himself.

"This is yet another minor annoyance as I take the time to recharge for another blast!" Gorrenwrath boomed. "Your own fates are already sealed!"

The sight of a small golden band spiraling harmlessly in the darkness of the eclipsed dimension announced otherwise. Armin, still concealed in shadow, saw the dislodged golden band, recognized it, and knew what he had to do.

The archer already had his bow in hand and fired off a single shot. That arrow pierced quite nicely through the Ring of Renecar's opening and sent the ring spiraling helplessly at Jovan. It was the Knight of Salvation's turn to restore his usefulness to the cause. With a mighty swing from the recovered Icarus, The Knight of Salvation sent the Ring of Renecar spiraling airborne and out of Gorrenwrath's grasp once more. A mystic burst of light from Talian not only illuminated the world of darkness but cast the ring into ruin.

At the ring's destruction, Gorrenwrath collapsed in his dark robes in the middle of the floor. The Trinity promptly sprang back to life and surrounded their enemy.

"The Ring of Renecar is gone from my grasp!" Gorrenwrath wept. With the loss of power, he crawled pathetically at the feet of the Trinity that he had once threatened to destroy.

"The source of Greatest Evil, born before all ages, has lived for all ages because of a ring." Armin chuckled. He then replaced his bow with his swords for a close quartered kill.

"You want to rejoin your precious Ring?" Helimslynch demanded, drawing up WarCleaver with renewed vigor.

Only the voice of the one man who should have taken the most satisfaction out of Gorrenwrath's demise stopped them. The Knight of Salvation's humility was restored to his voice and mannerisms once more as he made a final declaration.

"Gorrenwrath has lost." He declared. "The Ring of Renecar made him immortal. We shall let his renewed mortality take the man who was once ageless."

The Elf and Dwarf considered the request before Armin resituated his weapons in his belt once more. Helimslynch grumbled once more and began to begrudgingly replace WarCleaver.

"Hold, friends." Talian interjected, settling a hand on Helimslynch's shoulder. "We cannot allow a place of such evil to go unmarked."

"If Gorrenwrath will eventually die of age," Helimslynch declared, gripping tightly to WarCleaver once more, "then let us be responsible for the destruction of this dark prison!"

Armin drew his bow and quiver at the suggestion. Still, being nearest to the Knight of Salvation, he paused long enough to look to him for permission.

"If the Icarus were still whole, I would assuredly join you." Bourg chuckled. "Smash this imprisoning dimension. Spare the jailor's life for the day that natural causes satisfy your wish for his fate."

It was all of the permission that anyone needed to hear. Talian's mystic bursts, Armin's arrows, and Helimslynch's brute strength made short work of Gorrenwrath's dark dimension. Finally, the moment came that Bourg interjected once more.

"The dark dimension is destroyed and Gorrenwrath is in misery." The Knight of Salvation announced, "Let us return home…"

Eternal darkness gave way to daybreak and the Fellowship was situated at the peak of Mount Lyr once more. The dark dimension was a distant memory. Helimslynch was the first to shatter the silence of the relief that they were greeting a new sunrise. The Dwarven General, his life renewed by Gorrenwrath's magic but his heart pure, marched to the end of the peak. Here, he thumped his burly chest proudly and announced the new day.

"We have won a great victory, friends!" he bellowed to greet the new day and announce to anyone within a several mile radius about their triumph. "Most Holy and Noble Knight of Salvation, let me take your helmet, your armor, and your sword! I will gladly restore each to their former glory in the fires of Iron Mountain!"

"An unnecessary expenditure of your time and great talents, General." Talian insisted. "Observe."

With a sweep of her hand, Talian produced a radiant glow that soon surrounded Jovan Bourg. Once the glow of light was gone, there stood a Knight of Salvation whose armor glistened as never before. Such an arrival radiated promises of hope and peace for generations on Trina to adhere to. Before any question could be raised about its fate, the Icarus reappeared in its master's hand, fully restored.

"Bah; magic tricks!" Helimslynch snorted.

The Knight of Salvation turned on his heels. There rested his damaged helmet and body armor.

"Your original offer is not forgotten, my friend. Take these as precious metals to forge to your liking." Bourg offered.

Helimslynch snatched the metals, considered a clever retort, and genuflected gratefully before the Knight of Salvation anyway. Some distance away from the proceedings, Armin gazed off into the distance as if lost in thought. His bow and quiver of arrows were placed at either side of the archer and clearly within reach.

"Are you perhaps fixing to celebrate with us or would you shoot me in the back again?" Helimslynch barked, "Be warned; there be no more Gorrenwrath to restore what you've broken."

Armin reflexively jumped as if snapped out of his thoughts and whirled to face the source of the commotion. Due to the sudden interruption, his bow was instinctively back in hand.

"My apologies, Brother Dwarf; it was a great triumph for all of us." Armin observed, sheepishly laying aside his weapons. "But Mount Lyr remains in its lost glory. Why is that, Knight of Salvation? We crushed the Ring of Renecar, defeated its master, and destroyed Gorrenwrath's dimension. Yet, things on Mount Lyr remain unchanged."

The Knight of Salvation nodded in understanding of the question. There was an additional moment as he struggled to maintain his composure before he spoke once more.

"Mount Lyr was untouched by any hand of Gorrenwrath's destruction. He only placed his agent here." Bourg explained. "The downfall of Mount Lyr's former glory was due to the downfall of men. Gorrenwrath manipulated the greed and appetites of our politicians and church leaders until the day of their demise. However, the acts leading to their destruction were their own. The same rings true for poverty-stricken Nauros and the war-torn Church capital of Krill. The defeat of Gorrenwrath cannot restore that which was destroyed by man, even if by his manipulations."

Armin could only nod somberly at the observation. It did, after all, make perfect sense. Gorrenwrath's defeat had been but the first part of the Fellowship's job in repairing what his evil had destroyed. The job of restoring Trina from the untimely demise of war and poverty and restoring the world to the glory that it once represented was another case altogether.

"Talian, restore noble Swift and faithful Bob to our sides for the pilgrimage back to Krill. We must press forward to stop this Holy War at its place of greatest source." Bourg declared.

"You will each find that your steeds are waiting at the foothill of Mount Lyr in the desert of Scilia." Talian announced, "Perhaps I might also repair your face and body before you are presented before our people as our

Savior. Though I fear that I cannot repair the true damage that was done to your ear..."

"Then I will listen intently from the right ear just fine; thank you for the offer." Bourg interjected, "You have done much for this Fellowship. When all is done, return to Seraphic Forest. A great and noble falcon who helped me on this quest's very last leg faithfully awaits your return."

Talian gave the briefest nod and spread her magnificent wings to return to the majesty of the Seraphic Forest. However, she did not do so before her own somber concerns came to light.

"It was the greatest honor to serve with this Fellowship; but I have failed in the privilege." The Celestial Guardian observed. "I did not steer from the Ring of Renecar."

"The Ring of Renecar possessed many before you; and those who had failed in their mission *died* to their possession of the Ring." Bourg insisted, taking the Guardian passionately by both hands. "You have failed no one and I would be the first to gladly petition to wise counsel that we have each benefited from your restraint."

"I shall deliver the same report as the noble Knight." Armin vowed.

"And if they ask for a third, the General will speak for you too!" Helimslynch announced.

Talian afforded a slight chuckle, her spirits improving. With that, the Celestial Guardian spread her majestic wings and took to the air on her way back to the Seraphic Forest. Thus left the Knight of Salvation, Elf, and Dwarf standing atop Mount Lyr.

"We best restore our mounts." Bourg announced. "Gorrenwrath's defeat has not steered off the threat of Holy Warfare."

The heroes each repeated their vow of defense of Trina's shores and descended Mount Lyr. To everyone's astonishment, Bob and Swift really did await the heroes patiently at the mountain base. Helimslynch restored his place in the powerful pack animal's saddle while Armin and Jovan mounted Swift for the long journey home.

THE RETURN HOME

Krill's primary house of worship stood standing in all of its glory once more. Mother Superior could not have been prouder of the accomplishments of rebuilding. A ceremonial Mass in celebration of her own dedication to her craft was set to happen that very evening. In fact, Joto had already sent out the invitations. The glorious service would celebrate the hard work of the parishioners, support the Knight of Salvation in his continued works, and promote healing and unity between two rivaling factions. Still, this gathering was mostly to celebrate Mother Superior.

Evening drew over Krill and darkness settled, announcing but a few more hours until the celebratory service. The unbelievers took obvious exception to using the House of Ministry to celebrate its leader's personal successes that may or may not have had anything to do with her religion. Furthermore, this was an opportunity to make their own case as clear as possible in front of a large crowd. Several unbelievers settled around a smoking campfire, presided over by Darath Noar with satisfied determination. This would be the even on which the believers were made to understand their position.

"Make haste!" Noar ordered, "If we are to be welcomed into their Holy Place as believers, then we must *look* as believers. Only once inside their House of Deceitful Worship can we present our loudest case to the largest collection of high and mighty worshippers!"

A timid hand dared to settle itself on Darath's shoulder in the middle of his call-to-arms. He whirled to face his childhood friend and most loyal soldier, Pelos Lascar.

"To disturb the proceedings of their meeting of worship is wicked!" Pelos hissed to the man recognized as their movement's leader for confidentiality. "The believers harm no one whilst their soldiers are situated in their pews!"

"Then they will assuredly attack us afterward unless something is done tonight!" Darath barked, brushing his oldest friend's hand away and defeating the purpose of the act of disagreement being confidential as each of his followers glared at the two men. "These are the believers who murdered your brother. Yet, you offend me by speaking in their defense before our soldiers!"

"My brother was murdered by a *demon-servant* of Gorrenwrath!" Pelos reasoned. "I beg of you; to do as you plan will only provoke the ire of the enemy."

"Well, the Soldiers of the Cloth would have gladly murdered your brother if the beast hadn't beat them to him." Darath insisted, adjusting his tunic and his hair once more to closer resemble a man of humble religion. "We stand ready with weapons; let them be provoked! Do you ride with our cause, my brother, or would you prefer to situate yourself in the nearest pew?"

Before Lascar could answer, the disorder in the valley during a discreet meeting of preparation was answered by a louder commotion nearer to the church grounds. The unbelievers, each finishing the disguises that would welcome them into the Grand Hall, all glanced in the direction of the sudden crash. Mother Superior stood in an upstairs church window, looking proud of herself and tended over by her aide. The grounds in front of the church were littered by armored soldiers, carrying bayonet mounted rifles. Similarly clad soldiers instantly surrounded the valley and the personal meeting of unbelievers. Darath merely smiled in satisfaction and produced his own bayonet-mounted rifle from nearby.

"Darath, don't...!" Pelos insisted, placing himself in between the holy soldiers and their unreligious counterparts. A nearby gunshot, clearly meant for Darath, struck Pelos instead and Darath's leer only deepened. The religious had just proven his case for him, he was going to live to see the outcome, and the voice of dissent was silenced. Darath kicked aside the now useless body of his oldest friend and turned to face his loyalists.

"Soldiers of Humanity, the church has drawn first blood and has done so unprovoked!" he barked. "Let the Text-thumping, narrow fools shoot as many of us as they wish. They will only soak their Holy grounds in the blood of dissent! All that we need do is to stand our ground!"

At that instant, a giant sharp object came hurtling through the air and dove in the direction of where Darath had once been standing. The loudest voice for standing the ground of religious dissention instantly shrank back in cowardice. Believers and unbelievers alike were just as hopelessly confused as to where this new projectile's origins had been.

The unwelcome projectile sank squarely into the ground separating the unbelievers and the oppressors that had surrounded their meeting. As the campfire continued to glow and moonlight enveloped the ground, the blade situated in the ground promptly began glowing as if it were ethereal. Believers and unbelievers alike gazed upon the elegance of the radiant cross and dropped their weapons to their sides in renewed peace.

"People of Trina," a new voice interrupted the silent awe, "keep your arms cast down!"

Mother Superior knew that voice and craned her neck to discover a rider of radiant light approaching the church steps to address the assembled soldiers. Again, the forces of unbelief would escape just punishment because of her son's intervention. However, shouts of acclamation interrupted the doubts and despair welling up in Mother Superior's mind. Believers and unbelievers alike could appreciate all that the Knight of Salvation had done for precious Trina and the thought of warfare was gone in his presence. Granted that this was to be marked as *her* night to entertain adulations for her accomplishments, Mother Superior would have otherwise joined right in in celebrating the return of the Knight of Salvation. However, she would never the church's loudest dissenter. Joto peered over Mother Superior's shoulder and spied the arrival of the member of the Fellowship as well.

"Mistress," Joto announced, "your son has returned."

"Fetch the ring, red carpet, and best cloak and perhaps you should welcome him home properly.[5]" Mother Superior snapped.

Joto fell back from the church elder, crestfallen and stunned by her vicious words of her own flesh and blood.

"I am certain that he would much more appreciate such festivities if they were delivered by his mother, Mother Superior." Joto insisted.

Mother Superior gazed out over the crowds once more and determined that they were fully prepared to welcome the Knight of Salvation back to his home port in celebration. The forces of belief and disbelief alike had rallied behind respect for the Knight of Salvation and the Fellowship that followed him. Mother Superior could certainly do the same. What better reason to pack the church for celebration than in welcoming the Knight of Salvation home?

"Most honorable Knight of Salvation," Mother Superior called from her perch in the church's upstairs window to guarantee that she had an early audience, "welcome home to you and your allies. In these trying times, your efforts have spared Trina that Krill may abide in security through the actions of the Knight of Salvation[6]. I do apologize that not all of our worshippers have arrived for service yet but if you will perhaps wait..."

"Quite alright...mother." The Knight of Salvation interjected, removing his helmet to reveal the healing human face of Jovan Bourg, a simple farmer and one with a useless left ear besides. To gaze upon the face of a simple farmer, "Son of the Cloth" or not, stunned the believers They rushed to resecure the helmet that he would properly hold the crowd's attention.

"Leave the helmet askew!" Darath barked from nearby, halting the proceedings. "The Son of Bourg may address us as is."

Jovan nodded in appreciation and began once more.

"The Fellowship has returned following the defeat of a most vicious enemy." Bourg announced. "We have met Gorrenwrath face to face and his reign of evil has ended. His powers are lost and his dark dimension destroyed. Age will take him in time."

A cry of appreciation came from the surrounding people of Trina as a rush of bodies separated the Knight of Salvation from Armin and Helimslynch. As a few believers approached Armin and a handful of unbelievers accepted Helimslynch, it proved nothing compared to the crowd that now begged the attention of Jovan Bourg. Still, both members of the Fellowship forced a pair of smiles and nods of adulation for their true leader. Jovan Bourg had gathered together an Elf and a Dwarf to work together as part of an underlying Fellowship. It was his leadership and example that had them together in a bond of renewed brotherhood. That in itself was no small matter; and it only served additional praise for the man who had defeated Gorrenwrath. Amidst the rush of people, Xian Imor settled a hand on Jovan Bourg's shoulder.

"Welcome back into the fold, Son of the Cloth!" Xian announced. "Perhaps now you will aid the church in avenging the injured Viscar Halas, a great leader!"

"Or you will discipline the mighty church to leave others in peace until they can practice what their precious Book preaches!" Darath interjected.

Cries of acclamation and adoration over the Knight of Salvation's homecoming reduced themselves once more to shouts of anger and accusation. Armin and Helimslynch began to advance to deliberately place their steeds in between the forces of belief and unbelief. In anticipation of the oncoming riot, Mother Superior dropped a secret signal and the doors into the church entry burst open once more to reveal more guards. Still, the Knight of Salvation had seen enough and raised the Icarus heavenward for silence.

"Lay down your arms and listen to yourselves!" Bourg bellowed. "Gorrenwrath's reign of evil has *ended*; yet, the day of Trina's demise is no further away! I was summoned here to save Trina and *all* of its members. Now, my efforts are threatened to be for naught because of an evil inspired by *man*. Church, you ask me to ally myself with you and *strike down* the unbelievers rather than minister to them. Rebels, you seek my blade to silence the church on *your* behalf. I am The Knight of Salvation of the people. If any amongst you should cry to me in your pain, I am proud to hear you and defend your needs. Do not ask that I turn my blade against another on behalf of a war that *you* have created, friends. I have come to end this threat; not to participate."

"Your church began this war!" Darath barked.

"Then let the unbelievers be the first to lay down their arms and extend the hand of peace across the aisle." Bourg replied before the recrimination could be answered by an armed missionary. "Or those of you who represent the church. Since you are accused of *starting* this war, perhaps you wish to be the first to lay down your weapons and raise up your Sacred Texts for the unlearned in heartfelt ministry. Mother Superior, with your continued permission, I shall repeat my petitions once enough parishioners have assembled."

"Your petitions are unkind to this house!" Mother Superior declared. "Be on your way, Knight of Salvation, that we may celebrate Gorrenwrath's defeat and your return properly."

As Mother Superior went to disappear back into the church, a skeletal hand settled on her shoulder. The church elder whirled to face the somber, yet determined, face of Joto.

"Forgive my intrusion in this issue, my lady; but your edicts are *wrong* this time." He announced, confidentially. "We cannot fully celebrate the Knight of Salvation's return if the Knight of Salvation is disallowed from attendance. Open your church's doors to hear his words in full council. Believer and unbeliever alike shall be allowed into the most Sacred Grand Hall for such an occasion."

All was silent for a moment as Mother Superior deliberated how best to answer to the charges put forth by her farm servant. Then, the doors to the church fell open in an all-encompassing invitation to all whom had already assembled on the church grounds. Declarations of adulation entered the house of worship as the Knight of Salvation and his Fellowship entered the building first in preparation.

"HAIL TO THE KNIGHT OF SALVATION!"

"PRAISE TO THE *FULL* FELLOWSHIP!"

"LONG STAND NOBLE KRILL!"

The unintelligible shouts could only be answered by one voice. Though a smile of hope plastered its way to Jovan Bourg, the crowds deserved to hear what he said next.

"Pray, Sisters and Brothers, for the salvation of Trina." The Knight of

Salvation declared. He then situated the Icarus into the ground yet again before proceeding inside. He was backed by his Fellowship in leading all of the invited people. The church's doors were burst wide open in welcoming fashion and the Icarus cast its welcoming radiance over Trina for miles around. Gorrenwrath's manipulation had ended and the Knight of Salvation and his Fellowship were home. Furthermore, the open invitation to worship had momentarily pacified further bloodshed. For the moment, Trina's Salvation seemed like a plausible future once more. Such was a day for all of mammon to work toward.

EPILOGUE

Fair Trina, born in the earliest of ages as a great Paradise. With its lush plains and peaceful weather, no natural force could harm the ethereal beauty of such a world. Then humanity discovered the great beauty of Trina's shores. With the hope that humanity wished to bring with it came the proficiency to do evil.

The religious came first to Trina's shores. The human eye graced the planet's beauty and marveled in its magnificence. Truly such a creation had come from the Great King that humanity bowed to in highest regard. Believers built churches and houses of worship in which to sing praise of the beauty and glory of such a place. As they bowed in worship of such greatness, they would reach out to the surrounding community in an all-encompassing embrace to bring them in. However, the frustration and dissatisfaction of first stumbling upon a fellow person who did not share in the doctrines of the believers presented a degree of difficulty in their carefully constructed ideals.

The unreligious, drawn in by the charm and serenity of Trina, arrived next in search of a utopia of peace. The peace of their newfound utopia, however, knew very prompt limits. As each of the unbelievers was approached by a member of the believers promoting all that the churches knew, the unbelievers illusions of peace were shattered. Peaceful outreach became cold ostracizing leveled against those who did not worship as the church did. The sense of belonging in their own paradise dissipated. Ostracizing, rumor spreading, hateful rhetoric, and harsh judgment led the unbelievers to understand that their Paradise would not be a peaceful one so long as it was shared with the believers.

War became the answer that both sides took to with excessive earnest. The people who had disturbed Trina's shores sought not a utopia where shared ideas were welcome. Each side sought a Paradise devoid of differentiations in belief. Since Trina did not offer one, the people sought to make one for themselves.

It was the Holy War; pushed from one generation to the next and occasionally manipulated by the unseen Great Evil. He could only employ and amplify the human weaknesses of suspicion, hatred, and fear of that which they did not understand. It was a war of generations that had cost many lives and only a boy born of the believer and unbeliever could quell the hatred.

From the brinks of near destruction at the hands of war and Gorrenwrath, Trina now stands tall as a planet of peace once more. Its restored position as a utopia of peace is a long time in the future and will require the works of many hearts and hands. However, the sensation of the hope for the planet's possibility to reach the heights of peaceful utopia is renewed.

CITATIONS

1   "Behold, the days are coming," says the Lord, "That I will raise to David a Branch of righteousness; A King shall reign and prosper, And execute judgment and righteousness in the earth. (Jeremiah 23:5; NKJV)

2   In His days Judah will be saved, And Israel will dwell safely (Jeremiah 23:6a; NKJV)

3   For all that is in the world—the lust of the flesh, the lust of the eyes, and the pride of life—is not of the Father but is of the world. (1 John 2:16; NKJV)

4   so that the coming generation of your children who rise up after you, and the foreigner who comes from a far land, would say, when they see the plagues of that land and the sicknesses which the Lord has laid on it: 'The whole land is brimstone, salt, and burning; it is not sown, nor does it bear, nor does any grass grow there, like the overthrow of Sodom and Gomorrah, Admah, and Zeboiim, which the Lord overthrew in His anger and His wrath.' (Deuteronomy 29: 22-23; NKJV).

5   The parable of the Prodigal Son.

6   In His days Judah will be saved, And Israel will dwell safely; Now this is His name by which He will be called (Jeremiah 23:6; NKJV)

LANDMARKS OF NOTE

❖ **KRILL-** Krill marks the religious capital city of Trina. Inhabited by humans, the city houses the largest house of worship. Following the downfall of Mount Lyr, it has become the home of the leading voices of the church. As home to the leading voices of the believers, it is also the site of most bloodshed in the Holy War between the believers and the unbelievers who take exception to the church's excess authority over the daily lives of others.

❖ **DAWN VALLEY/TRESS-** Atop the mountain peak of Tress preside the Elf Lords, humanoids of mystic legend born with inherent beauty and natural authority. The Elves of Dawn Valley are only a bit beneath the Elf Lords and certainly viewed as above mankind. Due to their natural aesthetic perfection and leadership, the Elves are unfamiliar with the language of humility, quite often mistaking worshipping their own beauty with worshipping their Great King. Only an Elven archer and hunter, praised in Dawn Valley and shunned on Mount Tress, seems the least susceptible to delusions of self-confidence. However, this is only in comparison to other elves.

❖ **IRON MOUNTAINS-** A natural furnace responsible for forging many weapons and a natural hideaway for the Dwarven folks of disbelief. As excellent blacksmiths and mighty warriors, the Dwarves once found a common union with the forces of unbelief. Yet, even the forces of unbelief dismissed the dwarves back into the obscurity of the Iron Mountains. As a large and loyal union, the Dwarves proudly dismiss the idea of manmade religion from the very men who ostracized them and treated their physical differences as results of past sin. It would indeed take a Dwarf strong in his sense of loyalty and determination to ever join the Fellowship.

- ❖ **SERAPHIC FOREST**- Home of the Celestial Guardians of humanity sent forth from the Mighty Savior to watch over the people of Trina and offer their personal protection. They are as beautiful as the Elves and even exercise a degree of magic. However, the rules governing their powers are quite strict in terms of keeping a degree of humility and using their great powers for healing. An infraction to these rules results in a loss of power and majestic glory.

- ❖ **CALLISTRA**- Adjoined by the beauteous Callistra Sea, Callistra is a prominent fishing village harboring people and Elves alike. As fishers and trappers, Callistra's inhabitants naturally work for a living.

- ❖ **SCILIA**- The desert realm governing one side of Mount Lyr. The Callistra Sea presides on the other. The two are forever separated.

- ❖ **MOUNT LYR (LIAR)**- A place of fallen beauty and lost glory, Mount Lyr once served as a safe haven and undisturbed refuge for the powerful politicians and church leaders. As Lyr's people gave way to gluttony, greed, and arrogance, however, they gave way to death beneath an Unseen Evil; and their home gave way to ruin.

- ❖ **NARDOT**- A frozen purgatory set aside for only the very worst offenders. Those whose crimes are deemed unpardonable by man are exiled to Nardot to live out the pain of their last few moments before being entombed in ice forever.

- ❖ **NAUROS**- A village governed in poverty and patrolled by the believers. The innocent people of Nauros are born into a city of poverty. For their troubles, missionaries patrol the streets under the auspices of "ministry." Their actions instead separate families and orphan children through arrests on trumped up charges of "offending the cloth." Just as the believers, the unbelievers are determined to aid the downtrodden and ride to battle with the missionary soldiers. War and bloodshed only mount themselves on top of the inherent struggles of poverty and Nauros is no closer to freedom.

❖ **ZANTU-** A beautiful island Paradise hiding a very deadly secret. With its lush climate, beautiful shores, and enticing mist, many sailors were drawn to Zantu. None ever returned. Such beauty only gave way to forbidden desires, perpetual madness, and, eventually, apparent destruction of any mortal who visited Zantu's shores by way of the Callistra Sea or rivaling Polaris Sea.

THE PEOPLE OF TRINA

- ❖ **JOVAN BOURG**- The White Rider. The Holy Knight. The (White) Knight of Salvation. The Son of the Cloth. Many names govern Jovan Bourg as the son of Mother Superior, Martilla Bourg, and the elite soldier of the unbelievers, Captain Maxim Bourg. All that Bourg learned of pride in any and all religious works, he learned from his mother. All that he learned of humility and honestly assessing the works of the church and of mammon came from his father. Striving for only the best qualities of both parents and carrying the Icarus, a boy of humble beginnings must rise to become the Knight of Salvation, leader of the Fellowship, and, ultimately, the leading voice of peace on war-torn Trina.

- ❖ **ARMIN (ARE-MEAN) KINSTON (KINGSTON)**- The archer and swordsman. His hunting techniques have earned him the praise of the lower Elven castes as they realize that they have his respect in return. His ADOPTION into nobility has cost him the respect of the Elven Lords and he is disregarded by his royal family. When the time comes for the archer of humble beginnings to rise up as a member of the Fellowship, he must first learn to take up the language of true humility and true worship of a Great King; not just the gifts that he has received. As time passes on, he must also control personal desire before it consumes him to destruction.

- ❖ **HELIMSLYNCH (Helmslink)**- Proud, brash, cynical, loyal. He is the epitome of a Dwarf and one of their finest blacksmiths and generals. With a temperament as fiery as the furnace of Iron Mountain and a heart roughly the size of his home, Helimslynch has slung his mighty axe, WarCleaver, against the Great Evil in the past. He must now join forces with a group of believers, including a noble Elf, in defeating this threat once and for all.

❖ **TALIAN ARRACK (ERIC)**- Blessed as a Celestial Guardian, Talian shares in their beauty and use of magic. As their princess, Talian is more beautiful than ever and must struggle to maintain a level of humility above and beyond that of her fellow Guardians. Her wings allow her the gift of flight while her staff and tether whip provide weapons. Elion, the golden horned falcon is her guide. As to the most precious gift of her beauty, it may mark the downfall of her and Armin yet.

❖ **MAXIM BOURG**- Father and guide to Jovan Bourg throughout his youth until the father's death marking the son's twentieth year. A respected soldier and captain of the unbelievers, it was the father who taught Jovan to exercise humility. He would often be the one to chastise his negligence of the very doctrines that the church should teach him.

❖ **MARTILLA BOURG**- Mother Superior, the highest and mightiest of church elders. As a leader amongst the believers, Mother Superior has garnered the support of many worshippers presiding beneath her rule. To her dismay, the loudest voice against pretend religious oppression comes not from Darath Noar, the young, new leading voice of the unbelievers. Her loudest oppressor is the Son of the Cloth and eventual Knight of Salvation; a boy who is ashamed of his church practices when he was raised to uphold their traditions.

❖ **JOTO LINDAR**- Personal manservant to Mother Superior, either in her church or her mansion, and oldest confidant of the late Maxim Bourg. Joto is quite loyal in his duties to Mother Superior, though he does pray for the day that she will see the errors of the results of some of her practices. Since Jovan was born until the day that he adopted the mantle of Knight of Salvation, Joto was quite often a voice of reason and advisor to the boy.

❖ **VISCAR HALAS**- Tough, dependable, and respected rider of the "Missionary" Soldiers of the Church. Curiously, he led the missionaries into their charges more often with a trident and net than with a copy of his Sacred Text. Perhaps he understood the conflicting paradigms. However, one would never know to watch him go into the field and few would ever ask him.

❖ **XIAN (ZION) IMOR (EEMOR)**- The youngest soldier of belief and Halas's personal charge. In the event of Halas's injury in battle, it is Xian who must take up the mantle of leadership for the forces of belief.

❖ **DARATH (DARETH) NOAR (NO-ARE)**- Youthful leader of the rebel forces of unbelief. With a hot temper, a quick trigger finger, and a strong desire for personal praise and satisfaction, Darath has led many an attack against the church and her worshippers.

❖ **PELOS (PAYLOS) LASCAR**- Noar's oldest childhood friend, a man who recently lost his brother to the Holy War. He is consequently the principal means to many of the ends of Noar's schemes. However, Pelos has revealed a conflict of interest in his role as Noar's second-in-command more than once. One such act of divergence marked his grave and the opportunity for reunion with his lost older brother.

❖ **ORAN (AURIN) KINSTON**- King of Elf Lords, he takes great pride in his physical beauty and natural leadership as blessings from a Great Almighty. However, for all of the pride that he takes in his own gifts and his twin children, there remains little room for those outside of Elven royal birth.

❖ **TEMECAR (TEH-MUH-CAR)**- King of Dwarves and wry observer of Iron Mountain. He understands the ostracizing that all Dwarves have endured beneath the rulings of mammon and, under his tutelage, no Dwarf shall ever know such abandonment by a fellow Dwarf in their extended "family."

❖ **STRATUS ARRACK**- King Supreme of the Celestial Guardians. Arrack takes the powers and mission gifted to him quite seriously and the punishment for misuse under his guidance is great. His sense of loyalty to the cause of the Celestial Guardians prompted the release of Princess Talian to the Trinity's cause.

❖ **RUMIOS**- Servant of greed to the Great Evil. His own fascination with the manipulation of other's greed has resulted in a heightened degree of a sense of greed in himself. He utilizes a minimal means of magic, mostly involving generating serpentine beams that give birth to mystic cobras.

❖ **DAZ**- The former highest archbishop until the mantle was taken by Mother Superior. He is now the last remaining inhabitant of the ruins of Mount Lyr. So long as he pledges to the service of the Great Evil, Daz keeps his youth and strength and remains the last member of Mount Lyr. However, he can no longer contend for his former position and must live out his years in knowing that he is the last living member of Mount Lyr until the day that he has irreconcilably failed the Great Evil.

❖ **SILAX (Sigh-lax)**- The only living member of the frozen Purgatory of Nardot and its chief overseer. Silax is a demon of ice and annoyed servant of the Great Evil. When wicked Gorrenwrath disturbs Silax's rest, however, even Silax must comply and utilize the mists of slothfulness to drive off intruders or his wicked frost breath to cast them into the same frozen prisons as the sinners. In his preferred sedentary state, Silax blends in with surrounding walls of ice until he is awakened once more.

❖ **MYNOS**- Beautiful and wily enchantress of envy. Not often seen without the demon, Drax, a single touch of Mynos's hand or breath from her lips can awaken the covetous desires in any man. As a sorceress intent on manipulating envy, the foul enchantress is embittered by her own desires as well. Still, her own desires are not for Gorrenwrath's power. Her desires are reflected in possession of the Knight of Salvation's mind and heart as her own...

❖ **DRAX**- Huge, bulging, beastly, and grey, Drax may appear as a brute or hired muscle for Mynos for as often as he is in her power. Still, beneath his muscles, the demon also emits optic beams and deadly nerve gas in his breath. Still, even these are but mere weapons in his arsenal. His greatest weapon remains his intellect and the cunningness of a true hunter.

❖ **BLACK KNIGHT OF GORRENWRATH-** Demetrius Slade is a school aged rival to Jovan Bourg. In his later years, however, Demetrius returns as the Black Knight, charged by the Great Evil with all of the Knight of Salvation's weapons and much of his powers. Indeed, this rival is a dark mirror image of the White Rider and one who very much longs to boast of the defeat of his opponent.

❖ **DARK SISTERS OF ZANTU**

- o **MILANA-** The original member of the three and a fallen Celestial Guardian. Her "sisters" were crafted in her image of her powers. Milana remains their leader and bases her power off of the manipulation of wicked desire. Her manipulations are indeed the mightiest weapon in trapping doomed sailors to Zantu's shores.

- o **PHADE-** A sorceress of disguise magic. She most often employs her dark talents to pass for a desired love in the lives of her victims and drive them to madness, confusion, and their downfall into sin.

- o **ENSNARA-** A wily enchantress who uses mystic snares and trap devices to hold her prey in their new utopian prison of Zantu. She is most often viewed as the "youngest" of the bunch.

❖ **GORRENWRATH-** Unseen force of greatest Evil, his origins, immortality, and limits of his power are shrouded in mystery. He travels from planet to planet and casts them into doom through natural disasters. Still, when even his powers cannot destroy a world by natural means, he enlists his wicked agents to destroy the people of his chosen conquest through their own weaknesses. However, for all of the Great Evil's power over both nature and human emotion and all of his vicious disciples, is even he strong enough to cast Trina's Holy Fellowship to failure?